A VERY FAIRY FUNERAL

MISTBROOK MANOR COZY MYSTERIES

A.N. SAGE

OLIVERHEBERBOOKS

Contents

Chapter One

The one thing they don't teach you about handling the dead is how much time you'll spend in the presence of flowers.

There are flower arrangements, wreaths, and the odd bouquets family members bring to the stoop as some tremendous gesture of goodwill. Let's not forget the shrubbery that sometimes gets dragged in with the bodies, depending on who handled the sign-off. All of this is to say, they should really offer classes on gardening alongside the funeral director degree.

I have taken to keeping a good array of blossoms growing on the property of the Mistbrook Manor Funeral Home in case an occasion of the floral variety should arise. And believe me, it often did.

It was quite lucky then that Orchard Hollow, our

quaint little town, has a local undertaker who also happened to be a fairy. Yes, you heard correctly. I, Lyra Moore, am a certified fae from beyond the portal. Well, certified *might* be a stretch, but I tried not to get into that. What's important to note is, like most fairies, I have a bit of a green thumb. Which is why the roses around Mistbrook Manor are in full bloom, despite it being the dead of winter.

I touched a fingertip to one burgundy petal, and the flower shivered beneath my touch. The color of the rose deepened, and the stem stretched a little taller. Smiling, I dropped my hand, glancing at the briar before me. The roses, the Black Baccaras that overtook the entire cliffside property, were my favorite part of the funeral home. They drew me to this place when I first arrived in Orchard Hollow. Though the ley lines running under the town dragging in all sorts of supernatural creatures may have had a touch to do with it. Whatever the reason, the roses were why I stayed.

I couldn't get enough of the lengthy stems, the velvety texture of the petals, and the way they could darken to an almost black at the edges. Stunning.

Oh, and the job. Fairy or not, a girl has bills to pay, and since no one else was lining up to herd the dead for the town, I happily volunteered. It kept me busy and, most importantly, alone. People tended to avoid funeral homes.

"Will the monstrosities continue to multiply?" a monotonous voice asked from behind me. "Or are you opening a prehistoric attraction park I wasn't aware of?"

I groaned, my shoulders slumping in exasperation, and spun around. Perching on a garden bench sat Theodore, glaring at me with beady feline eyes. Unavoidable, since he was a cat. I fixed the large, furry gray feline with a frown. "How long have you been sitting there?"

"Since I realized you forgot my dollop of cream," the cat answered. "Honestly, Lyra, is it so hard to remember? It's the same every morning."

"You know, changelings are allergic to whipped cream."

The cat's eyes narrowed on me. "Do not remind me," Theo purred. "One of the perks of being trapped in this cat body is there is no shortage of the milky goodness. Thank goodness I'm not a pathetic human who swells up to the size of a hot air balloon after a lick of cream. Now, back to the flowers."

"Perhaps you'd be free of the paws and tail if you hadn't picked a fight with your friend in Assignments."

"I will not repeat myself again. Bartholomew is no friend of mine. And it is not my fault that his nose is so shapely."

My eyebrows hitched. "But did you have to point it out when he was proposing marriage to his girlfriend?" I asked. "If you kept your mouth shut, you'd be living your best life as someone's baby right now, and not stuck in my garden as a mangy cat."

That was the funny thing about changelings; they sure carried a grudge. While it was a possibility that the fae in question didn't purposely mess up Theo's assignment, and sent him to possess a cat body instead of a human one. There was also the chance that he could have done much worse. I'd heard of fae going so far as to flush out entire villages back in Fairy over a miscommunication. Theo had best count his lucky stars that all he got was an administration error that landed him inside a cat. Considering how rude the changeling was, there were days even I couldn't put up with him. And I was a green fairy. We were the calm and collected ones in the realm.

Memories of my homeland made the hairs rise on the back of my neck. I pulled off the ribbon holding my golden hair in place, and let the long locks spill over my shoulders. My breath fogged up the air, and I pulled on the tall neck of my sweater, bringing it all the way up to my chin. Back home, cold weather was contained in the Winter Court. It took me some time to adjust to the abrupt seasons on Earth, but once I did, I couldn't get enough of it.

My gaze landed on the cat. "Want to build a snowman later?"

"Have you been drinking?"

Chuckling, I applied my magic to a few more stems, then stood up, brushing off the snow from my jeans. In the distance, Mistbrook Manor loomed and beckoned me in. The old three-story Victorian home was a spectacle. Taller than it was wide, it appeared to be reaching high to the sky with scaly fingers. Sitting right on the edge of the cliffs that surrounded the town, it acted as a beacon of sorts, except without any of the warm light. Instead, the manor was a dark and gloomy structure, covered in black brick and bay windows that seemed to watch you from afar. Punctuated in color only by the rose bushes I grew on either side of the front steps and the matching red door between them, it was as ominous as what hid inside.

Though I supposed that feeling was saved for all funeral homes, no matter their appearance.

My gaze rolled over the manor, heart jolting. I was home.

Around the side of the house, the sound of wheels crunching gravel made me pause. There were no visitations scheduled today, and I had no notes from the hospital that someone was coming by, so I couldn't for the life of me imagine who it might have been. Nerves spiked inside my belly. I tamped them down.

It couldn't be him, not here, not ever.

With a town the size of Orchard Hollow, one never

knew who might pop in for a visit, but I had death on my side, and the visits were few and far in between. Unless there was a tragic accident I didn't hear about from the sheriff, I doubted it was anyone I knew. Even the paranormals steered clear of Mistbrook Manor, and that was saying a lot, considering that the lot of them had abilities that would frighten even the most powerful Fairy. When you lived in a town overrun by vampires, werewolves, witches, and warlocks, you tended to be on alert for uninvited guests.

My frown turned into a full-on grimace. "Who could that be?"

"Don't look at me," Theo said, skirting by me. He jogged to the kitty door, pausing to glance over his shoulder. "I wouldn't dare bring someone into your dreary home."

With that, he slipped inside, leaving me with the ghost of a fluffy tail and an empty back porch. Rolling my eyes, I unlocked the rear door and stepped inside. The warmth of the manor instantly defrosted my chilled bones. Around me, the familiar smell of peppermint and roses wafted into my nostrils. I inhaled it greedily. There really was no place like home, was there?

Ditching my wool coat on the antique hanger in the corner, I took a moment to brush away any remnants of dirt from my hands. The scent of cleaner clung to the air as I walked down the dimly lit hallway. Framed paintings of landscapes, their gilded edges catching the light from a chandelier overhead, kept me company as I marched past the living room and kitchen and toward the front of the house.

As I neared the front of the house, the door leading to the morgue in the basement caught my eye. I paused, jiggling the handle to make certain it was locked before moving on. Not that I expected anyone to break in to steal a cadaver—most people wouldn't dare—but one could never be overly cautious in my line of work.

The doorbell chimed a second before I reached the wide mahogany door. My pulse quickened as my gaze darted to the oval frosted window, where the blurry shape of a figure cast a shadow on the other side. Tucking a stray strand of hair behind my ear, I straightened my posture, plastered on a practiced smile, and pulled the door open.

"Oh!" I yelped in surprise. "Danny, hi. I wasn't expecting you today."

The mailman, Danny Widows, tipped his postman cap my way. "Afternoon, Lyra. Just trying to get ahead on my deliveries, with the storm on the horizon."

"Right, of course. They're predicting a bad one, huh?" I asked.

"Biggest storm of the year," Danny replied. He handed me a large box, then nodded in the direction of a second stack, this one so high the boxes teetered. "Doing some online shopping?"

I shrugged. "Unfortunately, it's all business related."

Danny shifted his weight from foot to foot, his eyes dancing around the front porch. He pulled at the neckline of his sweater and there was a flush in his cheeks that wasn't there a moment ago. I didn't need to use my fairy abilities to sense the discomfort in the mailman.

Widening my smile, I dipped my head to catch his gaze. "Something the matter?"

"Um, not. Nothing's wrong. I... Well, *we* were wondering if you want to join us for drinks down at the bar tonight." The shock on my face must have been evident, because Danny quickly added, "Carmen is throwing a big bash before the storm, and she told me to invite you. Says you're too cooped up here all on your own."

I chuckled. "I see. Thank you for the invite," I said cheerfully, "but I already have plans for the evening." I didn't mention that said plans included Theo and a monster movie marathon. "But you tell your wife that I will certainly pop in one of these days. No need to fret over me."

"This is Orchard Hollow, Lyra. All we do is fret."

His boisterous laugh echoed down the driveway and past the cliffs where it crashed into the sea, dying away in the breeze. Saying our goodbyes, I continued to shower Danny with false promises of becoming more social, until he got into his truck and drove off. . I felt my muscles relax as soon as he was gone and I was alone again. The buzzing in my head lessened and I could finally concentrate on counting the boxes to make sure everything I needed was secured. With the storm on the horizon, I needed to be prepared for anything.

Mentally, I counted and recounted the delivery, coming up two boxes short each time. Frustration clawed at my chest. In my throat, a thick knot worked itself out as I swallowed hard, folding my arms over my chest. With a few huffed breaths, I pushed the boxes into the foyer and grabbed my car keys.

"Be right back, Theo!" I yelled into the belly of the manor. "I need to go into town to get some supplies. Don't set the place on fire."

A hiss echoed from somewhere inside the house. Locking the door behind me, I flipped the sign telling visitors to return later and walked down the steps. It looked like Danny's wife was getting her wish, after all. The fairy funeral director was coming out of hiding. Ugh.

Chapter Two

By the time I completed my shopping, there were so many voices filling the sidewalks of Cliff Row that I felt my head might explode. I tried to stick to the shadowy side of the street and pressed close to the shops, but I was still getting shoulder-checked every few steps. Winter in Orchard Hollow was no joke. It appeared every tourist in the country came for a visit this week, the main street in town overflowing with bodies. To my right, the Rose Hollow Hotel blocked out a good portion of the street, and I could already see people piling outside the doors for the tour. The hotel was one of the more popular establishments of our small town, on account of it being haunted. Or fake haunted, depending on whom you asked.

A giant folding sign slammed into the ground next

to me. I yelped, jumping out of the way before I got impaled by the stupid thing. My eyes rolled over the chalk-drawn ice cream cones on the blackboard and to the man positioning the sign. The fridge-shaped burly shop owner wiped his brow—shockingly slick with sweat, considering the cold weather—and fixed me with an apologetic grin.

"Sorry about that," he said. "Didn't see you there."

That was the plan.

The man's face scrunched as he inspected me and I caught the slight whiff of magic in the air around him. I couldn't quite place his paranormal roots, but based on his size and shape, I'd wager he was a werewolf. My gaze rolled over him to see if I could spot a magical family talisman, but there was nothing that caught my eye. Some paranormals liked to wear their talismans around, refusing to part with them, and it was often a sure sign of their magical heritage. The talismans were rare though—passed down to the firstborn in every generation. From what I knew of the magic on Earth, every paranormal family had an heirloom. A locket, a brooch, a ring, whatever. At the birth of the firstborn in every generation, the members still alive would travel into the depths of the town to the ley lines, where they imbued their family talisman with parts of their own magic and that of the lines. The trinket was then passed on to the child to amplify their abilities. Since this ritual was performed every generation, the talismans packed a punch when it came to magic.

Which was why most hid theirs away and only brought them out when the occasion called for it. None of it mattered to me, of course. My magic was completely different from the paranormals in this realm. It was why it was so important for me to stay under the radar even from others with magical abilities. I was too different—and not in a cool, new girl way.

"You all right?" Ray asked.

I coughed into my mittens. "Oh, yes! And no worries, Ray. I should have paid better attention."

"You from around here?"

The sheer confusion on his face told me that I was doing things right in this town. The point was never to become Miss Popular; it was to blend in and keep a low profile. And if Ray didn't have the slightest idea who I was, even though I bought five jugs of Rocky Road from him last month, then I did my job. The ice cream was for Theo, of course, but that didn't matter right now.

I pulled the wool hat lower until it came down past my eyebrows. "Not originally," I answered ambiguously. "Well, enjoy your day."

Darting past Ray and his sign of sure death, I dodged people until I cleared enough distance between us, then slowed down. The smell of coffee from the local shop, Bean Me Up, wafted in the air, and my nose wrinkled. I was never one for caffeine, but the locals swore by the place. Word on the paranormal street said that a witch ran it, which would explain its popularity. Witches were particularly crafty with beverages, on account of all the potion-making. Perhaps I should give the place a go one of these days.

The sound of a car horn blaring made me immediately reconsider the concept.

I pulled on the shopping buggy I used to transport the missing supplies. My shoulder screamed in agony as I maneuvered the giant thing down the street and around people. Seriously, would it have killed me to park a little closer to the pharmacy? By the looks of where I left my car, it was beginning to look like walking home may have been faster.

Switching hands, I pulled on the buggy as hard as I could, counting the steps to keep my wayward mind at bay as I trudged toward the pickup truck. By the time I reached it, I was sweatier than Ray and huffing and puffing like I ran a marathon.

If only I didn't have to hide being a fairy in this realm. It would have been lovely to use my wings to get around, but unfortunately, otherworldly creatures were not welcomed here with open arms, so the wings had to stay magicked away, as were the rest of my special abilities.

Hopping over a fresh pile of plowed snow, I climbed

into the truck and tossed the receipts from the day in my glove box, then took off down the street. My thoughts swirled in my head as the events of the last hour settled into the crevices of my mind. It had always been so hard to be in large crowds of people in Fairy, and now here on Earth, that I couldn't stop the fog dusting my brain from taking root. Images jumbled together as my brain tried to grasp one solid idea. It slipped away, and I was left struggling all over again.

This is why you stay home, I told myself.

And why I left Fairy in the first place, since most fae were extreme extroverts, but that was neither here nor there.

I swerved around the twirling cliff-side road that led back to the manor. On my left, the sea crashed onto the sandy beach with a raging speed. The white caps on the water could be seen for miles, even from all the way up here. It was stunning if you didn't think about how dangerous the deep dark was. That was everything, though, wasn't it? Beautiful and terrifying at the same time. The road branched out into a fork ahead of me and I slowed down the truck, to make a decision. One way led straight to Mistbrook and the familiar comfort of home, the other—the Orchard Hollow Cemetery. Also comforting, strangely enough.

Before I could get stuck in a never-ending loop of double questioning myself, I turned the wheel and headed westbound. It took less than five minutes to reach the ivy-clad iron gates that sectioned off the cemetery from the rest of the town. Another ten minutes to park and walk the winding paths lined with weeping willows and tombstones. And yet the effort was worth every second because I was finally here.

My eyes adjusted to the light of sunshine streaming in through the leaves, and I inhaled a frigid breath. Before me, tall stone structures competed for real estate on the grassy knoll, the mausoleums of people long gone. Most of the families who owned the buildings didn't even live in Orchard Hollow anymore, so this stretch of the cemetery was mainly abandoned. It was why I loved it so much. The peace only the dead could bring was addictive.

Wind trilled in my ears as the weather picked up and the sun dipped behind the copse of trees on the horizon. I closed my eyes to take it in. Tears burned behind my lids from the storm circling me, and I had to wiggle my nose so icicles didn't take claim over the skin inside.

"Why, in bloody hell, you find this place relaxing is beyond me."

Adrenaline carved up my spine, the hairs on my neck standing straight. I turned around slowly. Letting out an exasperated sigh, I looked down the length of the cat's body perching on a tombstone before me. "You know, one of these days you're going to sneak into my truck, and I'll lock you in there for the night."

"Don't threaten me with a good time," Theo retorted. "What has you tied up in knots, anyhow?"

"Nothing important," I admitted. "Town was extra busy today."

The cat's tail whipped over his face, and he pawed at it with a hiss. The fluffy appendage fell away, stroking the stone of the grave he occupied in nonchalant movements. Eyes narrowing, Theo said, "It would help your means if you took the time to blend in a little more. Make a few friends. Breathing ones."

"Ha! And what would you know of making friends?" I asked with a snicker.

"I'll have you know that before my current predicament, I was quite the popular fella."

Rolling my eyes skyward, I buttoned up my coat collar and looked past him between two tall mausoleums. It was impossible to see from here, more so to anyone without paranormal magic, but I knew it was there. My skin crawled. Stomach churning, I breathed warm air on my frozen hands. "May as well reinforce the darn thing while I'm here," I muttered to myself.

My boots crunched the snow underneath as I cleared the path between me and the portal to Fairy. Above my head, crows croaked as though they also knew the terrors hiding behind the doorway I approached.

Shadows crept over my feet from the buildings surrounding the portal, and a shiver tripped down my spine when I reached the exact spot the portal stood in. My teeth chattered.

"It's not going to fail," Theo said, galloping to stand beside me.

I shrugged. "Can't be too careful."

"You realize there has not been a Portal Fairy in centuries?" he asked. "You, Lyra Moore, are an anomaly. No one can reopen the bloody gates to Fairy except you. The lock you placed on them will hold."

When I didn't reply and only stood trembling, he added, "He won't find you."

I scoffed. "How can you be so sure?" I asked, my bottom lip quivering. "The Shadow Court Prince is as resourceful as he is vicious. I doubt he was pleased when the wife arranged for him ran off a week before the wedding."

"And yet the portal has held all these years, and he has never made an appearance," Theo offered. He walked between my legs. His tiny paws padded softly on the snow, leaving an index of perfect beans in their wake. Sometimes, it was easy to forget that he wasn't a cat and was, in fact, a changeling fae of some three hundred years of age. That is, until he said things like, "If you ask me, you should have slit the prince's throat before you traipsed off. Your father's too, for arranging the marriage in the first place."

I lifted a leg and stepped over him, making sure to kick a little bit of snow into his whiskered face.

"My father was a desperate man trying to save a flailing court," I told the cat for the thousandth time, but who was counting? "And I could never hurt someone. That's not the type of fae I am. Green Fairy, remember?"

The cat's brows shot up into his forehead. "Remind me, was everyone in the Summer Court so pathetic or were you special?"

This time, I didn't hold back. Throwing my foot back, I yeeted as much snow as I could collect on my boot onto the rude fluffball. The snow hit him square in the face, and he buckled back, shaking it out while hissing up a storm in my direction. He hopped around on the mound for a good minute in order to clear the clumpy mess from his fur, then shot a death glare in my direction before scurrying back to the truck.

His tail pointed straight to the ground and his ears tucked back as a final show of feline rage.

Chuckling, I brushed whatever snow stuck to my pants, squared my shoulders, and walked toward the portal. *Best to get this over with.* I stood in the center of the portal with the sun setting behind my back. Sweat beaded down my neck and rolled into the collar of my sweater. The cold drops were a constant reminder of the skin I wore, the human form I took on to blend into the world I escaped to. My fairy appearance wasn't all that different, unless you counted the wings, the sparkly pearlescent skin, and hair that grew flowers from its locks, depending on my mood.

But everything else was a dead copy.

I glanced around to make certain I was alone, checking the cemetery thoroughly. When I was convinced no one had followed me, aside from a rude cat, I cracked my neck and got to work. My fingers warmed as I reached for the invisible barrier of the Fairy Realm. Before my eyes, the air rippled when my magic connected with the magical lock on the doorway. I concentrated on pouring as much of my energy as I could into it, fortifying the magic already there.

The first time I created a portal, I had no clue what I was doing. I was a small child, and opened the darned thing in the middle of the hallway in Father's castle while I was playing. Luckily, only my mother saw me do it, and she guided me on how to close the doorway before anyone else came around. She told me it was an honor to be a Portal Fairy, and a task I should not take lightly. She also told me that if my father ever found out my secret, he would use it to his advantage to help our court. So, it was best to keep my mouth zipped shut about my special abilities.

I followed her advice for centuries—that is, until the marriage incident. My heart jolted. I hadn't thought of my mother in years.

Watching my magic swirl around me in iridescent ribbons of energy made tears burn the rear of my lids. No matter how much time I spent in this realm, I sure missed Fairy.

"Can we get a move on? My paws are ice."

Arms falling heavily to either side, I spun around to face Theo, who waited impatiently at the edge of the barrier. I blinked away the wetness in my eyes before he could make a snide remark about me crying. Forcing a smile, I pulled my magic back into my body and shook off the remnants of it with a shrug.

Looking at the cat, I tightened the belt of my coat and walked away from the portal. "How about a movie and snacks?"

When the cat nodded, my mood brightened. Earth wasn't so bad after all. At least it was calm and peaceful here.

Chapter Three

"Why is she going upstairs, Lyra? The killer is obviously going to chase her?"

Theo moaned and groaned from his side of the red velvet couch, his chubby form draped dramatically over the cushions like an underwhelming stage actor. Half his body was buried beneath a plush blanket that had seen better days, though it was the fine layer of gray fur he left behind that truly grated on my nerves. Every time he rolled from one side to the next, I could practically hear the fabric screaming for mercy, while I worked hard to ignore the mess. At this point, finding a corner in the manor untouched by cat hair was akin to hunting for treasure without a map.

On the screen, the movie's heroine bolted into a bathroom, her frantic hands slamming the door shut with a desperate *thud*. Theo's groans turned into a muffled snort of disdain as the killer effortlessly kicked it back open, sending it ricocheting off the frame. I leaned forward, the flickering light from the television lighting up my face. The scene played out in high tension, but the absurdity of it—the killer's perfect timing, the victim's poorly chosen hiding spot—drew a sharp laugh from Theo. His smug grin peeked out from beneath the blanket as if he was some all-knowing critic of bad horror tropes.

"What did I just say?" Theo screeched.

I shook my hair, the blonde waves falling free of my scrunchie immediately. "You do realize that if she left the house, there would be no movie, right?"

"There would be a better movie," Theo replied. He rolled his golden eyes and pawed a piece of popcorn into his mouth. "We should have watched the other one."

"May I remind you that you said you'd rather die a fiery death than watch the movie I suggested?"

"I am only three-hundred and twenty-seven years old, Lyra. I do not have memory problems."

A high-pitched scream tore from the television as the movie took a turn for the worse. The spectacle made Theo break into a monologue about modern cinema, and I took the moment to sneak out of the living room under the guise of refilling the popcorn bowl. As much as I loved the cat—though I'd never tell him that—I needed the peace and quiet the kitchen offered late at night. Theo was a lot to handle. Enough so that I sometimes contemplated planting Foxglove flowers in parts of the property to get away from him. The gorgeous stems, while pretty to look at, were atrociously toxic to changelings.

In the living room, the cat continued to complain, as I slipped away into the dimly lit hallway. The heavy oak door creaked behind me and the smell of polished floors wafted up with my every step. The walls, lined in dark mahogany paneling, led me toward the kitchen, which overlooked the backyard of the estate. In the dead of night, the only light in the manor was cast from the flickering wall sconces, and it created a somber atmosphere that lent perfectly to the overall mood of the house. I passed the small settee beneath the staircase and rearranged the frilly pillows atop it. My face scrunched.

Cat hair. Again.

Floorboards groaned beneath my feet as I rounded the corner and stepped into the kitchen. The space was modest compared to the grandeur of the rest of the home, but it was one of my favorite spots. With its cool stone floor and massive cast-iron stove, it was like stepping through time every moment I spent in here. When I moved in, I added brass pots and pans and antique wood furnishings to further bring out the charm of the room. Between these touches, and the flowers I usually had arranged on the window sill above the porcelain sink, it was too cozy for words.

I stepped toward the stove and turned it on, the kettle already filled with water for the tea I had each evening. While I waited for the water to boil, I prepped the leaves—a mixture of herbs I dried from my garden—and took inventory of the pantry to make sure we weren't missing anything important. By the time the kettle screamed to be turned off, I had an entire list ready for my next trip into town.

"Did you fall through another portal?" Theo yelled from the living room.

I shook my head. "Coming!"

Right as I stepped out of the kitchen, the calm silence of the manor was interrupted by a loud, boisterous rapping on the front door. I stopped in my tracks, the tea sloshing over the edge of the cup and soaking into the carpet. Glowering, I set it down with trepidation and made my way across the house. As I passed Theo, still perched on the couch, I ignored the choice words he shouted at whoever dared to interrupt our evening.

Rising on my tiptoes, I peered into the keyhole, the frown on my face deepening. I slid the gold chain off the wall hinge and unlocked the two locks. The front door groaned as I slid it open, revealing a uniformed police officer. The young man tipped his ball cap with Orchard

Hollow's police force logo embroidered on it my way. "Sorry to interrupt your night, miss," he said. "I have a last-minute delivery from the Holbeck General Hospital morgue."

I craned my neck to see past his wide shoulders where an ambulance stood parked in my driveway. The flashing lights illuminated the front yard, colors of blue and red dancing across the single oak tree on the property. It made the thing look like it was about to perform a circus act right there on the edge of the cliff. Or like I decorated for Halloween ten months too early.

I struggled to smile.

"What was so urgent that the morgue couldn't wait until morning?" I asked. "Lyra Moore, by the way. Officer...?"

"Samuels," the cop replied. He extended a hand, and I shook it briefly. "Holbeck General, a few towns over, is going through renovations. Our hospital is landing their facilities for the month, but they haven't been able to accommodate every case. Most of the bodies on site have been claimed by family and local cemeteries already."

My brow creased. "What about this one?"

"John Doe. No one seems to be able to trace who it is."

"Really?" I asked, my curiosity piquing. It was rare that an unidentified body showed up on my doorstep, especially from several towns over. In a place the size of Orchard Hollow, everyone knew each other. There were no John Does here. "All right. Well, let me prep the morgue and you can get your guys to wheel him in. Give me some time to get everything ready. I wasn't expecting anyone tonight."

The officer grinned toothily and crossed his arms, leaning on the wide banister of the porch. "Of course. Take all the time you need, Miss Moore."

I was about to close the door when the officer cleared his throat at my retreating back. Spinning around, I turned to face him, quirking a brow.

"You should know this one is odd," the officer said.

"Odd in what way?"

His lips pressed into a thin line. "You'll see. Guy was found in the park down by the old port. No sign of foul play, and the hospital has no idea what could have happened."

"No one knows how he died?"

The officer shrugged. He rubbed the rear of his neck, his skin creasing. "They're saying heart attack, but I don't know."

"What makes you think it wasn't?" I asked.

"Call it a hunch. He was sitting down on a bench when they found him, taking a break of sorts. It was bizarre." He glanced over his shoulder at the ambulance. "Well, I'll let you get to it. I'm heading back to the station, but the paramedics have all you need. Have yourself a good night, Miss Moore."

I watched him walk away, his heavy boots echoing in the night. My stomach twisted into knots, a tight, uneasy feeling that wouldn't let go. It was impossible to tell what the officer thought my definition of a good night was—probably something mundane like a quiet dinner or a movie, which was what I was attempting to do before he interrupted. He had no idea that good nights didn't exist in my world, not anymore. At least not nights where I could let my guard down. One thing was certain, though: my actual night was officially over, and not in a peaceful way.

They weren't kidding when they said the dead never slept. Or, they didn't in Orchard Hollow, it appeared.

Chapter Four

Fluorescent lights buzzed overhead as I worked on preparing the body for burial. Most people didn't understand the care one needed to take to ferry the dead to their next destination, but I respected the importance of this part of my job. Every detail counted, even for someone without a family claiming him.

I looked over at the man on the steel slab, my brows inching closer together. "Who are you?"

"If you're expecting him to talk back, you're further gone than I thought."

Glancing over my shoulder, I fixed Theo with a thunderous gaze, then turned back to the body. Behind me, the cat rummaged for something on the singular desk in the morgue—snacks, no doubt—knocked over several pens, then made a snide remark before leaving. With the basement empty save for me and John Doe, I got back to work.

I moved methodically, as I had done hundreds of times before. Gently lifting and moving the deceased as I prepared him for his final resting place. The surrounding room was stark and clinical, with the faint scent of formaldehyde mixing with fresh linens. It was a smell I had gotten so used to that I almost craved it when I was in other parts of the house. Creepy to most, I supposed.

Soaking a soft cloth in warm disinfectant water, I proceeded to clean, paying close attention to anything that might be out of place. Not that the hospital made an error in judgment or that the police missed evidence; it helped to be more thorough, just in case. There were plenty of known cases where undertakers discovered crucial evidence during the preparation process that helped solve cases.

I frowned.

Not a case. A simple embalming.

Getting through the remainder of the steps, I hummed as I applied touches of makeup to the man's porcelain skin. Even for someone deceased, his skin was impeccable. It didn't have the usual tinge of blue that formed when life ripped away from the human body, and instead glowed as though he had stepped fresh out of a spa. His brown hair was neatly trimmed, and there was no sign of a five o'clock shadow, suggesting he was cleanly shaven right before he died.

I inspected the rest of the body. No dirt under his nails. No piercings or tattoos. And he appeared to be in remarkably good shape, like he worked out regularly. Slowly, I removed the thick gold chain from the man's wrist. My eyes flicked to the expensive suit folded on the chair by the desk.

Whoever this man was, he was well off. Very well off, actually.

I wiped my damp brow with the back of my hand. The surgical gloves creased on my skin and goosebumps crawled over my body. For some reason, I couldn't shake the feeling that something was off about the body in front of me. The death, though very believable, struck me as odd, and I couldn't quite put my finger on why. Theo often said that *Timescape* vision was a hidden fairy ability of mine, but I knew that wasn't it. I couldn't see the future as my mother could. Now perception, that was a skill I had developed to the extreme, since it helped with my current job in the town.

That was all this was, I convinced myself. I was reading too much into details that weren't there.

A sharp clamor upstairs jarred me stiff, the noise piercing through the quiet basement like a thunderclap. My heart gave a jolt, but I forced my hands to remain steady as I finished my work. I glanced down at John Doe—his pale, lifeless form stretched out beneath the light of the exam table. A chill slid down my spine, though it had nothing to do with the body. This wasn't right.

I pulled the white sheet over the body, the fabric rustling with the same sound as crunched paper. Peeling off my gloves, I tossed them into the trash with a flick, and turned the overheads off, their low hum leaving my mind. The sudden silence was unnerving, but there was no time to dwell on it. Agitation gnawed at me, building with each passing second.

Theo.

He knew better than to interrupt me while I was working. My patience, already threadbare, snapped like a brittle twig as I stomped up the basement stairs, my footsteps echoing with growing irritation. My breath came in quick bursts, fueled by the tension simmering right beneath the surface.

Reaching the top landing, I paused for half a heartbeat before tearing through the manor. The dim light of dusk filtered through the large, arched windows, casting long, skeletal shadows across the floor. The old house moaned from my hurried steps, the wooden boards creaking as I moved from room to room, my eyes darting left and right. I swung open the cupboard doors and peered beneath every chair, muttering under my breath with each step.

"Where are you, you little rascal?"

Theo had vanished. He usually hovered nearby when I was in the basement, but not today. A deep scowl tugged at my jaw as I checked the living room, the kitchen, and even the showroom—the latter being his favorite spot, since he somehow managed to creep into the caskets on display despite my disapproval. Still, no Theo.

Where could he have gone?

Another noise made me jump, my butt slamming into a side table with enough force to knock over the vase sitting atop. I groaned. Luckily, the vase stayed intact, but it would take some time to clean up the water from the carpet. Shaking my fist, I looked down the darkened hallway. "Theo! What are you doing?"

"Me? You're the one clambering about in the dead of night."

I froze at the sound of the cat's voice behind me. Twisting slowly, I took in the sight of Theo, freshly awoken from sleep. He sat on the bottom step of the stairs, his bushy tail swinging. My eyes narrowed. "Were you upstairs this entire time?"

"Where else would I be at this ungodly hour?" Theo remarked. He nodded to the floral catastrophe. "Doing some late-night flower arranging?"

"You didn't make a noise just now?"

The cat shook his head. "For the millionth time, woman, I was asleep. What are you talking about?"

Nerves pricked my bones with tiny needles, sharp and relentless. My legs stood frozen in place, the weight of dread pinning me to the spot. Tingles ran up and down my arms in an erratic rhythm, a silent alarm my body couldn't ignore. If it wasn't Theo, then what was it I had heard? The sound had been subtle yet distinct, a shuffle or scrape that didn't belong. An animal, perhaps, but we never got wildlife all the way up here on the cliffs; the terrain was too inhospitable. And birds wouldn't be knocking things about like that. The thought lingered: unless it wasn't an animal at all. Something—or someone—was out there.

As soon as I thought about it, fear dragged at my spine. My heart slammed against my chest as I made my way toward the front of the house where the sound came from. Shivers tripped down my spine. My trembling hand reached for the doorknob. I paused. Taking stock of what was around me, I reached for the closest thing to a weapon I could find.

"A feather duster? Really?" Theo complained from under my feet. "You are truly deranged."

I rolled my eyes. "It is only a precaution. In case someone is out there."

"Oh, yes. You'll give them a good dusting. That'll scare them off."

Nudging him away, I wrapped my fingers around the handle of the duster, ignoring Theo's mockery. Slower than molasses, I fought against the terror coursing through me and opened the front door. Wind slapped at my cheeks instantly. My skin burned and my eyes watered from the harshness of the attack. I sputtered, white-knuckling my weapon.

Swinging the duster around, I checked the front porch.

Nothing.

I stepped outside on shaky, liquid legs. My bones seemed to have evaporated from my unnecessary fear, and I felt immediately foolish when I was greeted by more emptiness beyond the porch. Loosening my grip on the duster, I walked down the front steps and inspected the remainder of the property. A smile tugged at my cold lips.

"False alarm, Theo!" I yelled out.

"I don't care!" the cat replied.

There was little else to do except admit defeat and head back into the house. With the moon high in the sky and brightening the snow gathering over the pavement driveway, I realized the lateness of the hour. To my right, the oak tree groaned and creaked as the wind swayed it from side to side. Snowflakes fell on my forehead. I grinned, tipping my chin up to gaze at the full moon overhead. With no one here, I felt the freest I had in ages.

Before I could chicken out, I let my coat fall away and rolled up the back of my sweater. With a few fairy words—an incantation to remove the glamor I placed on myself—I let my wings pop out. They shot from my back so fast it was as though they had been waiting for this exact moment. I sighed. What a relief it was to be truly me, if only for a passing moment. The light of the moon made the pearlescent skin shimmer as I moved, and before I knew it, I was frolicking in a childlike happy stupor in front of the manor.

I was still giddy when my eye glossed across a disturbance in the snow I hadn't seen before.

Repeating the incantation, I placed the glamor back on the wings and they retreated into my body. My skin shivered as I bent down, fingers grazing the footprints left in the otherwise undisturbed snow. Since it wasn't snowing when the police left earlier, these were new. My eyes flicked to the falling snow reflecting in the moonlight. Very new.

Scanning the area again, I stood up and headed inside. The rear of my neck prickled as I stomped up the stairs, as though someone was watching me. I knew it couldn't be true. There was no one there; I made sure of it. Yet I couldn't shake the spooky feeling gnawing at my brain.

Someone was here, at Mistbrook Manor. And they left before I could catch them snooping around.

I locked the door and double-checked the locks and chain, then pulled aside the curtain to peer out. Somehow, it didn't seem as peaceful as it did a few moments ago. I shrugged. "It's probably nothing," I told myself.

But I still checked the locks again before going to bed.

Chapter Five

"Earth to Lyra! Anyone home up there?"

A whooshing sound jarred me from my thoughts. I turned right as a flying object came barreling into my face. My hand reached up to smack it away, but I was too slow. The slimy flat surface collided with my cheek, squeaking in that way that made people's skin shiver as it slowly slid down my face and fell to the table with a smack. Nausea shot up my throat.

"Is that a piece of ham?" I asked Theo.

Sitting in the kitchen across from me, the cat licked a second piece of sliced meat. I didn't know how he did it, but the menace managed a wicked grin before devouring the ham piece. "I called your name several times."

"So naturally, your next solution involved slapping me in the face with meat slices," I said.

"Naturally."

My eyes narrowed, the disgust coming back tenfold. "Ew. Please tell me you didn't lick that one, too."

"How else would it gain traction through the air?" Theo replied. "Blame it on science."

Picking up the nasty weaponized meat with a napkin, I tossed it in the trash, then set off to wash the dishes. The breakfast I ate gurgled in my belly, and my body fought against early onset anxiety. After a restless night spent tossing and turning, I could not get what happened out of my head. But that wasn't the worst part. What had me in knots was the body the police officer dropped off.

My brow scrunched in concentration as I scrubbed the pan.

"All right, you have my interest piqued," Theo remarked. "What has you so agitated this morning?"

I splashed water on the pan with too much force, and it blasted out of the sink to smear the countertops with soapy bubbles. Growling, I turned off the tap and spun around. "How can no one know him?"

"What?"

"The body," I explained. "John Doe. How can no one know who he is? There aren't that many people living here, and yet not one person can identify the body? It's bizarre."

The cat's ears perked, his head tilting sideways. "This is why you're upset? It's a stranger, Lyra. Why do you care so much?"

Typical changeling response. "I care because no one should be buried alone. It isn't right." I bit my bottom lip, the truth of how I felt burning a hole in my chest. "After I left Fairy, I knew I would be on my own. That if something were to happen to me, there wouldn't be anyone left around that would know about it."

"You and John Doe are not the same."

"We are, but that is not the point," I corrected. "It didn't matter that I would be alone. I could handle it. Prefer it, actually. But I also left Mom behind. With him. Trust me, if she were to die, my father wouldn't blink twice before remarrying. And I won't be there with her in the end."

The cat stayed quiet for so long I thought he fell asleep with his eyes open. If not for the slight sway of his tail and a single twitch of the whiskers, I would have checked for breathing. After what seemed like an eternity, he licked his paw and brushed it over the matted fur on his head. "You can always go back."

"If I return to Fairy, I will be forced to marry that murderous prince at best and hanged for treason at worst."

"Right. Well, best to make the most of your time here then," Theo said. "How about a little gardening to get your mind off the cadaver?"

I rolled my eyes in exasperation. "Please don't call him that," I said. "And I don't think even gardening will do the trick today."

"Thank the fairies, because I don't think I can handle you smelling of dirt right now. I have the worst case of a sensitive nose."

My eyes widened, an idea sparking to life.

"One, that's not an actual condition," I told the cat. "And two, I'm going out for a bit. You gave me an idea that might help ease my mind. Hold the fort while I'm gone."

Theo flashed me his canines and hopped off the table, running out of the kitchen with a whisper of "No, thanks."

Leaving the other dishes for later, I shrugged on my coat, grabbed the keys from the antique hook near the door, and headed outside. With the sun blazing high above, the day seemed warmer and much more inviting, a massive improvement to last night. I started up the truck; it sputtered to life as I rolled it out of the driveway and headed into town. By now, I knew there was only one thing that could get my mind to stop spinning: finding out who John Doe is, and letting his family know what happened. If I couldn't be there for my own flesh and blood, I certainly could do so for others.

My eyes flashed to the rearview, watching Mistbrook Manor shrink on the horizon. There was only one logical place to get answers, and it was a fifteen-minute drive away.

The Orchard Hollow police station was a stark opposite to the rest of the town. The lobby of the station was modest and unwelcoming, with concrete floors and chairs lined against gray walls that had seen better days. A vintage clock ticked quietly on one wall, next to black-and-white photos of the town's early law enforcement groups, giving the space an out-of-touch feeling, considering there were only three hanging. I tried to make out the faces but couldn't recognize any of them. There was an old rotary phone on a side table. I wondered if anyone still used it, or if it was there to add to the mishmash decorations of the place. It was there to put people at ease, no doubt, though it did quite the opposite. I kept waiting for it to ring, like I was in a horror movie.

The smell of coffee wafted in from somewhere deep inside the belly of the station. My stomach pitched violently from it. Everything about the station put me on edge, as I supposed was the intended purpose.

I walked to the reception desk with a hurried step and tried to avoid making eye contact with the randoms in the lobby. Anyone who landed themselves in the police station this early in the morning was harmless, of course. The people slumped in the chairs were likely brought in after too many drinks at the local bar, or other minor infractions. The lack of handcuffs was a sure give-away that I was correct, as were the snores filling the station lobby.

When I reached the main desk, my brow furrowed. It appeared to be abandoned. I was about to turn around and leave when a head popped up from under the desk. The receptionist, a woman in her fifties, pushed her gold-framed glasses up her nose as she settled into the creaky office chair. "Morning," she said, her voice gruff. "What are you here to report?"

"Oh, um, hello. I'm not reporting anything."

The woman arched one brow at me. "Did your pet run away?"

I shook my head negatively.

"Someone stole your mail? Broken street sign?" she continued to fire off. Her face darkened a few shades. "Please tell me this doesn't concern a dead body."

"Well, actually..." I stopped. "I'm Lyra Moore, the funeral home director over at Mistbrook Manor. One of your officers dropped a body off last night, and I was hoping to ask him some questions."

Her face scrunched up in concentration and she tapped the end of a pen on her chin, thinking. Suddenly, her eyes widened. "Right! Officer Dryer," she said excitedly. "I was off shift for a few days and am still catching up. You know how this town is, never a dull moment."

I didn't know how to break it to her that I had no idea how the town was since I worked hard to avoid the majority of it. Though that didn't mean I didn't know what was happening. News traveled fast in Orchard Hollow, even when you kept your head in the sand. Our small town has had its share of excitement lately, with deaths skyrocketing and bodies piling up. I knew because, for the most part, I was the one that handled them. Word on the street—well, on the paranormal street—was that a witch by the name of Piper Addison had been making a name for herself, helping solve crimes in the town. I'd never met the woman, but anyone who was using their magic to help humans was A-Okay in my books.

I smiled at the receptionist. "Hopefully there won't be any more incidents any time soon," I said. "But is Officer Dryer around?"

"Let me check for you, dear."

She disappeared down the narrow corridor on the right side of the desk, humming the entire time. I couldn't quite place the tune, but had the feeling it would be stuck in my head for the rest of the day, anyway. Tapping my shoe against the concrete floor, I waited for the woman to return, keeping my eyes down. When ten minutes passed, I craned my neck to see where the receptionist vanished to, but all I could see from here were closed doors and more concrete. My gaze flicked from the corridor to the desk, eyes snatching on a manilla folder.

It was stamped with yesterday's date and the words John Doe in red ink at the top corner.

Urgency thrummed through me as I realized what it was. This was the man's file. The one that now lay in the freezer of my morgue. My fingers itched with the need to reach for the folder. I fought the curiosity tooth and nail. What was it humans said about cats and curiosities? I should ask Theo when I return—he'd know.

When the receptionist still failed to return, I couldn't take it any longer.

With a quick swipe, I grabbed the folder from the desk and laid it open before me. My eyes scanned the few pages inside hungrily. As predicted, there was a short police report and notes from the hospital stapled to the back of it. I read through the report, finding nothing new that the officer didn't mention last night. The deceased had no identifiable traces on him. No ID, no wallet, not even cash. Perhaps he was robbed prior to dying? Or after?

I continued to peruse the notes, periodically checking for the receptionist. Much like the police report, the hospital had little to say. They marked the death as a heart attack with no findings of foul play. I was about to close the folder when a scribbled note in a rushed hand caught my eye.

"Toxicology report pending," I read aloud.

Why were they running a tox report if the death was ruled natural? Odd. I made a mental note of it and closed the folder, placing it back on the desk the way I found it. Behind me, one of the sleepers choked on his own spit and coughed loudly, making my nerves hike up. I turned to see the man wipe drool off his chin, then roll over in the chair to continue snoozing. What a champ.

Twisting back to the desk, my heart leaped into my throat at the sight of the receptionist sitting there. I clutched my chest. "Geez! You scared me."

"On edge?" she asked, rearranging her glasses.

"Something like that," I replied. "Did you happen to find Officer Dryer?"

The woman's lips pressed into a thin, apologetic line. "Sorry, dear, he must have left without me noticing him. I can get the sheriff for you if you prefer?"

My gaze flicked to the folder.

"No, thank you," I said. "I'll stop by another time. It really isn't all that urgent."

"I wouldn't imagine so. Can't get any deader, right?" the woman joked. "Give us a call ahead of time so you don't waste the drive next time."

Thanking her, I made my way out of the station, giving the sleepers a wide berth as I passed. I spent the entire drive back home thinking about the file folder and the bizarre toxicology report the hospital ran. It didn't add up. There would be no point in checking for toxins in a heart attack case, not unless they thought something was amiss. As I swerved up the cliff-side road toward the funeral home, I continued to roll ideas through my head. Perhaps I was wrong not to examine John Doe more thoroughly. There was no question about it—if I wanted answers, I had to look at the body again.

I parked the truck and jumped out before the engine cooled. My boots padded the snow as I ran up the driveway and onto the porch, my fingers grazing the roses climbing the trellis. Reaching for my keys, I started to open the door and froze in my tracks. My pulse thundered between my ears. Heartbeat racing, I stilled my shaky legs and took a step backward.

The front door was ajar.

Chapter Six

The thing about someone breaking into your home was not so much the fear of catching them in the act, though that is a valid worry, but it is the not knowing who was inside. Or, in my case, *what* was inside. Ever since I escaped the death sentence of my arranged marriage to an actual monster, I had looked over my shoulder. Every shadow could have been the Shadow Court Prince, every lone footstep at my back, his guards, every sound that didn't belong... You get the idea.

The fae as a whole were not the most loving creatures, at least not the royal bloodlines, but the Court of Shadows was the worst of them all. The place was full of treacherous creatures that lived to torment, and they were led by a family of murderers and thieves. The oldest prince was no exception. In fact, he was the worst of them all. Unfortunately, he also possessed the most powerful magic in all of Fairy, and had his eyes set on me for years. When he offered my father power and riches in exchange for my hand, I begged for my freedom. My words fell on deaf ears, as they often did with my father.

Leaving was the only way I could survive whatever the prince had planned for me.

And now, it appeared he had found me at last.

Saliva pooled in my mouth as I stared at the small sliver of light piercing through the opening of the front door. One thing was for certain, I did not leave it unlocked, and Theo had no opposable thumbs. Someone else was here, someone uninvited. Terror raked my bones with its vise grip as I worked to gather the courage to step inside. Keys in hand, I flipped them around and poked a few out between my fingers, making myself look like a makeshift Wolverine wannabe. Since there was nothing else around to defend myself with, unless I counted the thorns of the rose bushes, it would have to do.

Rolling my shoulders, I sucked in a quivering breath and slowly pushed the door open wide enough to slip inside. My heart continued to race as I scanned the front hallway of the manor. Relief swelled in my chest when I found it empty. I stopped moving, breathing even, and listened for a sound. The house was as quiet as ever, with no signs of a disturbance. I dared to take a few steps forward; the hand holding the keys high in front of my face. Twisting my head, I checked the front sitting room. Empty.

My shoulders dropped. Slowly, I checked out the library, kitchen, living room, and the den I converted into a waiting area for people visiting the funeral home. That only left one more space on the main level of the house—the casket display.

Straightening my spine, I walked the length of the hallway, my side brushing against the wall for added support. Sucking in a deep breath, I blinked twice, then twisted the handle and burst into the room. Darkness overwhelmed my senses, and it took my eyes a moment to adjust to the lack of light. I felt for the light switch, my knees knocking. As soon as the light turned on, I was pushed backward by a thick, heavy mass. My back slammed into the door, closing it with a slam. Butt sliding to the floor, I shoved at the mass of fur and nails attacking. When I finally freed myself from the clutches of the annoying cat that jumped me, I was more annoyed than afraid.

"Theo! For the love of Fairy! What are you doing?"

The cat shook off its paws and jumped from my chest to land on the floor with a soft thud. "Protecting myself, you heathen."

"Is the intruder still in the house?"

Theo cocked his head and cast me a sideways glance. "What intruder?"

"Whoever broke in. Isn't that why you jumped me?"

"Oh. Sure. Let's go with that."

I narrowed my eyes at him and breathed out. "Never mind. Come with me."

With Theo treading softly behind me, I walked to the grand staircase, my shoulders stiff. My gaze traveled up the stairs, and I paid close attention to see if I could hear noise coming from the second floor. Winding between my legs, Theo's whiskers twitched. "Is it a paranormal?"

I shrugged. Most paranormals in Orchard Hollow were impossible to recognize. Because of the need to hide their true self from humans, their kind had taken to staying so off the radar that they didn't even recognize magic in each other. There were instances where some were more obvious about their abilities, going as far as wearing magical family talismans in broad daylight, or using light magic. But for the most part, no one knew who was paranormal and who wasn't. Except me, of course. Green fairies weren't the same breed as the rest of the magical beings in town. Because I came from another realm altogether, I had a way of sniffing out magic. Literally. A bittersweet smell usually filled the air when a paranormal was nearby and I was the first to recognize it.

I assumed all fairies would have the ability. Then again, I have never had the chance to prove my theory, since I have yet to meet another of my kind here on Earth.

Pointing my nose up, I gave the stairs a quick sniff and grunted. "Can't tell from all the way down here."

A loud clamor shot through the house. The walls shook from the sudden sound and my ears buzzed. I looked at Theo, mouthing, "The morgue." His ears perked in response.

The cat darted away from me and toward the locked door of the basement. Readying my metal key claws, I took after him, my boots hitting the floorboards hard enough to make them vibrate underneath. On my panicked arrival home, I had completely forgotten to take off the snowy shoes, and I cursed myself for the slicked wet prints I left in the wood as I ran. If I wasn't dragged back to Fairy today, there would be a lot of polishing in my future.

Lips tight, I raced toward the rear of the house. When I reached the basement entrance, I skidded to a stop mere inches from Theo. His little paw pointed at the open door and the light emanating from below. With a tight nod, I took the first step down into the morgue. My skin cooled to the touch as the frigid air of the refrigeration system clawed up my body. Every inch further down sent shivers up my back and neck, and my muscles twitched with worry.

A low curse drifted from inside the morgue as the clatter of metal falling filled the room. Whoever was down there, they'd knocked over my instruments. Wonderful.

As a precaution, I shimmied my shoulders and pulled some of my magic to the surface. I couldn't do much except grow a killer garden and open portals, but being a green fairy didn't come without its perks. Since I could control the natural world, I could use anything in nature to my advantage. If I concentrated hard enough, I could probably work the few plants I kept in the morgue as a defensive shield.

Flashes of the shadow prince's evil grin filled my mind. No way would that be enough to stop him.

You have to try. Don't go down without a fight.

I continued to murmur words of encouragement as I walked down the stairs and into the morgue. Stepping into the cold room, I dropped my magic. "Huh."

The man standing with his back to me was most definitely not the Shadow Court Prince. He wore worn-out jeans and a vintage leather jacket that rippled around the obvious muscle of his arms. Shaggy brown hair peeked out from a newsboy cap, and though I couldn't see his face, I felt the strain of his emotions from where I stood.

I gave Theo a little kick of acknowledgement and the cat responded with a frustrated hiss.

The man spun around, realizing he wasn't alone for the first time since I stepped foot in the morgue. His cheeks flushed, sharp brown eyes landing on me. "Hello."

I glanced at the man, then at Theo, then back at the man. Clearing my throat, I motioned for the stairs. "Who are you, and how did you get inside?" I asked. Quickly adding, "I already called the police."

"There's no need to worry, Miss..."

"Moore," I replied, my face twisted. "You broke into my home. There is plenty of need to worry, I suspect."

The man pulled at the collar of his shirt, making his jacket squeak. "I assure you, I mean you no harm. My name is Detective Flynn," he said calmly. "I work for King City Police, and am in town investigating a recent death. I believe the body was delivered to your funeral home. And to clarify, I did not break into your home. I came into a public place of business. The door was open."

He's lying. Why is he lying?

I stepped backward. Boot hitting against the bottom step, I coughed into my hand and fixed the detective with a serious glare. My fingers twitched, and I had to shove them in my pockets, so he didn't catch me worrying my nails. Biting the inside of my cheek, I tried to appear as relaxed as possible, though my brain was working overtime. "Do you have some form of identification?" I finally asked.

Detective Flynn reached into his jacket and my heart stopped. Noticing my worried face, he slowly pulled out a leather wallet and opened it to flash me a police-issued badge.

"Thank you," I said. "You can never be too sure these days. Now, what's this about a body?"

"An unidentified man's body was dropped off here last night," he explained. "It may be related to another case I'm working on."

I forced a meager smile. "Right, of course. There was a John Doe delivered, but I don't see how it could relate to anything. The man died of a heart attack."

"You didn't find anything to suggest foul play?"

"I wasn't looking," I answered stiffly. "I'm sorry, shouldn't you be asking the hospital these questions? They are the ones who examined the body."

A spark caught in his narrowed eyes as he regarded me from head to toe. The detective shifted his weight like he was trying to figure out whether to run or stay. His broad shoulders hiked up, and he gave me one last glance before looking around the morgue. Supposedly satisfied by whatever he saw, he nodded once and walked toward me.

"I'm covering all my bases," he said, brushing past me toward the stairs. "As you said, you can never be too careful. I'm sorry if I scared you earlier. It was never my intention."

I gritted my teeth. "No problem. I'll walk you out."

As I marched behind him to the front door, I could not stop thinking there was something amiss about the detective. What police officer breaks into a funeral home and then proceeds to lie about it? If there was, in fact, a case Detective Flynn was working for the city, he would need the proper paperwork to examine my place without me present. Surely he could have waited until I was home to ask his questions. The entire interaction put me in a frenzy, and I couldn't wait to get the man off my stoop and out of my life.

I opened the door with a little too much force and all but shoved the man out of it. The detective cast me a solemn glance before tipping his ridiculous hat. "Thank you for your time, Miss Moore."

"Sure. Good luck," I replied. I didn't wait for him to turn around to slam the door shut.

Twirling away, I leaned against the wood as if the mere weight of my body would make the detective leave faster. When I heard his footsteps retreat, I finally allowed my bones to melt.

I looked down at Theo, who followed me out of the basement. "Where was his car?"

"Whose? The cop's?"

"Yes," I answered. "If he was here on official business, why not park in the driveway like everyone else does? I didn't see a car coming in and nothing on the drive over."

"Unless he walked."

I quirked a brow. "All the way up here? I doubt it."

My head twisted back to the door, mind racing. Before I could change my mind, I grabbed a thick scarf from the front closet and my purse from the floor. Bundling up, I peered through the peephole to make sure the detective left, and opened the door.

"Where are you going now?" Theo asked.

I looked at him over my shoulder. "Be right back," I said. "Off to do something very foolish."

Chapter Seven

Trailing the detective was proving to be a far trickier endeavor than I'd anticipated. My only frame of reference came from a lifetime of crime dramas and Hollywood's portrayal of private investigators, none of which prepared me for the real thing. Still, I refused to back down, gripping determination tighter than my nerves. I maintained a careful distance, making sure to keep to the edges of the path, my breath puffing in little clouds in the chilly air. The winding trail was uneven, dotted with loose gravel and damp leaves, and my footing faltered with almost every step. It was akin to navigating a sheet of ice.

The detective, on the other hand, moved with ease. His brisk pace sent up small scuffs of dirt with each step, his boots striking the ground. His broad shoulders were set, his stride steady, as though he belonged here—or at least knew where he was headed. How did he know the area so well? I clung to the rough bark of nearby trees for balance, using their towering forms for makeshift cover.

Every time I glanced up, I half-expected him to glance back, but he didn't. He pressed forward, oblivious—or so I hoped. My heart thudded in a rhythm that felt deafening against the hushed silence of the road. With every crunch of a misplaced step, I winced, certain my clumsiness would give me away.

The strange man walked for several minutes, finally disappearing behind a bend in the road. Moments later, the roar of an engine sounded. I stuck close to the shadows falling from a large oak, watching his car speed out onto the road.

That was why I didn't see his car earlier. He had it hidden from sight, another reason not to trust him.

Spinning on my heels, I ran back up the road and started up the truck, pulling it out of the driveway faster than I had ever before. I followed the direction of the detective until I spotted his car on the road, then slowed down. Staying a safe distance away, I drove after him, my hands white-knuckling the wheel. The entire scene was out of a mystery novel—absolutely bonkers.

When the detective finally veered off the main road, my mouth gaped.

"The cemetery?"

Why was he going in here?

I followed behind until he stopped the car and parked. Allowing the detective to walk farther ahead, I climbed out of the trunk and dashed after him. My boots made a mess of the snow-covered trails as I darted around tombstones to keep up yet stay out of sight. Even though we were the only people in the cemetery, I still felt that I was being watched the entire time. It was an unnerving gnawing at the back of my head that kept me glancing over my shoulder every few steps.

The detective did not appear to have the same reaction to the cemetery, and trod ahead with the assurance of someone who had spent many days in and out of the place. I racked my brain for any memory of him in all the times I'd paid the portal a visit, but nothing came to mind. He made a sharp right turn and my heart sank. The stranger was taking the long way to the portal site, I was sure of it.

If he wasn't from Orchard Hollow and was only here following another case, how did he know about that part of the cemetery?

Nothing about this man added up, and the more I saw, the more I disliked him. When he reached the exact place I stood in yesterday, my entire body convulsed.

What are you doing here?

A part of me half-expected him to sprout wings and

disappear into the portal. Instead, he walked right past and darted into the shadowy opening of one of the mausoleums. My eyes raked over the worn-out etching at the top. Starling. The family name didn't ring a bell. Then again, none of them did. Why was this specific mausoleum important to him?

I gave the area a once-over before running in after him. As I entered, I noticed two things right away. One, the inside of the mausoleum smelled of dead rats and even deader people. Two, the detective was nowhere in sight.

Spinning in a circle, I checked every nook and crevice and came up empty. Where could he have gone? I was standing in the middle of a ten-by-ten box, not exactly a great place for hiding.

"What in a fairy's nose?"

I checked again with the same pathetic results. Walking around the perimeter of the mausoleum, I clung close to the walls and searched for any hidden compartments I may have missed. I doubted the man vanished into thin air and I didn't smell magic on him, so he couldn't have used special abilities to whisk himself out of here. Detective Flynn had to be here somewhere. I just had to look more carefully.

It was then that I noticed it. The tiles on the floor farthest from the main entrance were shinier than the rest of the mildew-stricken flooring. I inched closer, pulling out my phone to shine a light on them. I was right. They appeared to have been freshly polished. No, that wasn't correct. Not polished but worn in, as though someone had slid them across another surface.

My head jerked left and right, looking for a miracle. I pressed my hand to the wall and tested every brick in the way I had seen adventure seekers do on television. My palm caved into one brick and a definitive click cut through the silence of the mausoleum. In a flash, the floor shifted, tiles sliding under each other to reveal an opening.

"No fairy way," I whispered. "Theo is going to be so jealous."

Craning my neck to see clearer, I rolled my gaze down the winding stone stairs that led into the dark abyss below. My teeth were chattering even though it wasn't cold here. Steeling my spine, I blinked twice and took one small step toward the opening. "Here goes nothing."

I descended the narrow stone steps, each one winding in a tight spiral around the core center. The air grew colder with each step, and the faint smell of rot seemed to seep through the walls. My hand trailed along the damp stone for support. Below, a flickering light illuminated just enough for me to keep going. I could have used the flashlight of my phone, but I didn't want to alert the detective to my arrival ahead of time. Or at all.

I looked back at where I came from. This likely wasn't my brightest idea.

Regaining some courage, I kept on. When I finally reached the bottom, my breath caught in my throat. Before me stood a gargantuan iron door, its surface etched with symbols I didn't understand. There was nothing but stone on either side of me and the staircase at my back, so I knew Detective Flynn must have gone through here. Hesitantly, I stepped up to the door and gave it a push. The iron creaked and moaned as the door slid open to reveal a room far larger than I expected.

The space I stood in was cavernous and dim, lined from floor to ceiling with towering bookshelves that bowed under the weight of countless tomes. At the center of the room stood a large round table made from dark oak, and around it, high-backed chairs were tucked in and ready for use. Above the table, a chandelier made of wrought iron hung low, the light I saw earlier filling the space. Books upon books lay atop the table in a particular sense of order.

My gaze traveled around the room. "What is this place?"

A throat cleared to my right.

I jumped, yelping. I spun around so fast my hair swung and slapped me on the mouth. Spitting it out, I blinked away the confusion and took in the person that dragged my attention from the strange space. Detective

Flynn had lost his hat, and raked his fingers through his tousled hair as he watched me in surprise. But that wasn't the part that had my heart racing. What worried me most was that he wasn't alone.

Three people flanked the detective's sides. Their watchful gazes studied me carefully, as though to gauge the danger I presented. A ridiculous notion since I was the one trapped in an underground...what, exactly? Lair? Library? I had no clue, but I knew it couldn't be anything good.

"I see you didn't check to make certain you weren't followed," the man on his right side said.

He was the oldest of the group, somewhere in his late sixties, if not his seventies. His tall, gaunt frame gave him an almost skeletal appearance, with sharp angles where his bones seemed to press against his pale, papery skin. His expression remained perpetually somber, as though his face had forgotten how to smile decades ago. Deep lines etched around his eyes and mouth. His silver hair, neatly slicked back without a strand out of place, shone in the dim light, adding to his severe appearance.

Dressed in a black three-piece suit, he looked as if he'd walked straight out of an old *film noir*, or an extra from a spy movie. If spies were old enough to be someone's grandfather, with a stiff, formal posture and weary patience that only the elderly could truly master. A gold pocket watch dangled from his vest, gleaming as he absentmindedly flicked it back and forth, a rhythmic gesture that seemed to serve no purpose other than to fill the quiet with its soft metallic clinks.

The detective next to him frowned. "How was I supposed to know she'd be behind me, Mortimer?" he asked. "This is a first."

"Not your first mistake though," the young, petite woman remarked. She pushed her thin black frames higher up on her nose, and ran slender fingers through curly dark hair. Her sharp, inquisitive gaze stayed glued to me when she added, "This time it's a real mess-up."

I fought the urge to tell her off, though I couldn't quite grasp why I was so angry. A sharp heat twisted in my chest, but I swallowed it down, forcing myself to stay calm. Instead, my attention shifted to the third woman in the group, the one who had remained cool and composed amidst the rising tension. She stood out from the others, not only because of her demeanor, but because of her appearance.

Slender and poised, she had long black hair that cascaded in loose, effortless waves down to her shoulders. Her sharp, almond-shaped eyes were focused but unreadable, as if she saw far more than she let on. Unlike the other three, who were draped in dark, dreary fabrics, this woman had a lot more charm. She wore a flowing floral dress, a soft mix of pastel hues that contrasted with her dark hair. The long, billowing sleeves swirled around her wrists as she shifted her weight, as though she was out of another era.

When she caught me watching her, her full lips quirked at the edges, pulling into a subtle grin. It wasn't mocking exactly, but there was something behind it—something sharp, as though she could read every thought flickering behind my eyes.

I cleared my throat awkwardly. "Um, hello. Sorry to intrude on whatever this is, but..." I folded my arms over my chest. "...what is this place?"

The detective worked his jaw. The older man grimaced. The firecracker with the short hair growled deep in her chest, and I'm pretty sure cursed me out a little, while the quiet one only continued to glare at me.

"I supposed there's no point hiding it now," the older man, Mortimer, said.

My brows slanted. "Hiding what?"

He waved a hand over the bizarre space we filled, his eyes crinkling. A warmth spread over his face, and his gaze rolled over me slowly. "We are the Grim Wardens," he said ominously. "Welcome to our home away from home."

Chapter Eight

If someone were to ask me to list the most pivotal moments of my life, I could do so in a single breath. Leaving Fairy. Buying the funeral home. And today.

But this moment seemed to eclipse all the others.

I stared at the four strangers in front of me, my mouth dry and my mind racing to make sense of what I was seeing. Disbelief turned to unease, then spiraled into outright panic, as the weight of their silent glares pressed down on me. My chest felt like a vise had been clamped over it, each turn of the invisible bolts driving the air from my paper-thin lungs.

The room, an expansive underground chamber, seemed alive in the worst way. It was shrinking—impossibly, alarmingly shrinking. The dark stone walls wavered as if they were made of smoke, then solidified again, only closer. They pressed inward, creeping with a determination that felt more terrifying than architecture should.

The books lining the shelves rattled violently, their spines vibrating against the wood in a warning. I half-expected them to leap from their places and hurtle toward me, each thud of their quaking bindings matching the thunder of my pulse in my ears.

My body trembled uncontrollably, the vibration seeping into my bones. My feet felt rooted to the floor.

"Wonderful, you broke her," a snarky voice remarked.

I shook out my anxiety and faced the young woman, who had one eyebrow raised high enough to touch her hairline. My skin crawled from her icy glare. "What are the Grim Wardens, exactly?" I finally uttered.

It was Mortimer who spoke instead. The man folded his arms over his chest and turned his serious gaze on me. I instantly felt like a child being scolded. Mortimer seemed to have that effect, because even the detective—who I very much doubted was one—shrank in size.

"To better explain who the Grim Wardens are, it is best to start with how we came to be," Mortimer said. "It may come as no surprise that the four of us have things in common."

Wait, are they fairies?

"We all share the same profession."

Ah. Right. That makes more sense.

Noticing the confusion plastered on my face, the old man smiled, his teeth sparkling. "That's right, Miss Moore. Everyone in this room is an undertaker. Ellie Blackwood and Rosemary Singh run the funeral home over at Graceling Heights. Mr. O'Malley...Finn is the morgue director for Holbeck General Hospital. And I am the proud owner of the Coalfell Funeral Home."

I took note of the town names he mentioned, realizing they all circled around Orchard Hollow. In fact, the cemetery was smack dab in the center of all their locations. I wondered if it was why they chose to meet here. But mostly, I wondered how no one knew the secret lair they used existed.

As though reading my mind, the fake detective motioned around the room, saying, "This mausoleum has been a part of my wife's family line for many generations. The Starlings originated in Orchard Hollow, but unfortunately, there is no one left to carry on the line." He paused, his face darkening. "Jenny's grandfather was a bit of an eccentric, and built his library beneath the tombs. It seemed to be a natural place for us to meet."

"Does Jenny know about your group?"

Finn's jaw worked itself out. "Jenny died five years

ago. But to answer your question, she did. It was her idea to join."

A deep-rooted sadness banged against my ribcage. Finn may have deceived me and broken into my home, but to hear that he lost someone so important to him broke my heart. I had seen my fair share of widowers at the funeral home, and nothing could quite compare to that loss. Though Finn appeared to be cool and collected, I knew that a piece of him was missing. It was a terrible thing to imagine.

"I'm sorry for your loss," I said.

If he heard me, he didn't reply. Instead, Finn took one small step back to give Mortimer room to come forward to finish the story. A notion the older man was more than happy to receive, since he all but leaped into action. His face was animated, and his hands moved quickly as he spoke.

"Years ago, a body arrived at my funeral home," Mortimer explained. "The death baffled the local police, who spent months working the case with little success. After a while, the case went cold, and other matters took the attention of local law enforcement away from the woman. Ally Cambridge."

I pressed a hand to my chest. "That's awful."

"It is, but sadly, it is also quite common," Rosemary added.

"Very common, indeed," Mortimer agreed. "While

the police forgot all about poor Ally, I never could. So, I took it upon myself to dig deeper. After a lot of work that had nothing to do with my position as an undertaker, I found out how the woman died...her family finally had closure. It was the single greatest moment of my entire career."

My brows knit together. "And it made you start a secret club?"

Mortimer chuckled.

"Not exactly," he said. "It was a few years before our group came together. After what happened with Ally, I continued to do my job and keep my nose down. That is, until Ellie and Rosemary showed up on my doorstep. It seemed word got around about what I did, and they had an odd case of their own that they wanted to solve. It was no surprise that after working in concert, we knew we had to keep going. We were helping people in ways we never could as simple undertakers. It was an honor to bring peace to the families left behind." His eyes landed on me. "As I'm sure you could imagine."

He was right. I truly could imagine how amazing it would feel to give John Doe's family the closure they needed. I nodded slowly.

Gaze darting to Finn, I asked, "How did you get involved?"

"That's a story for another time," he answered.

That's not at all ominous.

My head ached from the onslaught of information. How was this even possible? A secret society of crime-solving undertakers was unbelievable enough, but to find out their lair had been beneath the portal to Fairy this entire time was mind-boggling. It was too much to be pure coincidence and a part of me wondered if I didn't walk in on some elaborate setup created to lure in a fairy in hiding. I raked my gaze over the group. Nope. There was no way these people were anything but human. A fae wouldn't be hiding out underground. The fairies were a proud bunch, and if they were gallivanting around town solving crimes, rest assured, they'd want the glory that went along with it. Whatever this was, magic didn't touch it.

I took a stab at a smile, but it came out lopsided and awkward.

"Why were you skulking around Mistbrook?" I asked Finn.

The burly man shrugged. "We needed information on your John Doe."

"To solve a case?"

A throat cleared behind me. I followed it to Rosemary, who was leaning against a towering bookshelf a few feet away. She tossed her shiny locks over her shoulder and closed the book she held, tucking it under her arm. The sleeve of her dress swallowed it whole. "To solve *his* case," she said. "We don't believe that he died of a heart attack."

"How did you…" The words fell away from my lips. I deadpanned on Flinn. "The hospital renovating their morgue. That's where you work, isn't it?"

He nodded.

"That's how you knew about the heart failure and where to find the body. Where to find *me*."

Another confirming nod.

"And?"

His eyes rounded. "And what?"

I shook my head in frustration and rubbed my aching temples. "Did you get what you were looking for?" When he didn't answer, I added, "Your hospital ran a tox report. What did it say?"

The entire room shifted to look at me. Each undertaker took a step forward, encroaching on my personal space and making me wish to turn invisible. Too bad that wasn't a fairy skill I could connect to, because if it was, yours truly would be gone in a blink.

I rolled out my shoulders. "You did know about the report, didn't you?"

"We did not," Ellie said. She turned away from me and opened a laptop, furiously typing frantic words into it. A moment later, she glowered. "She's right. There's a report, but it hasn't come back yet."

"They must have run it recently or else I'd have seen it in his file," Finn said.

"How did you know about it?" Mortimer asked.

I crooked a smirk at him. "The police had a file on John Doe," I answered. "I may have accidentally read it."

There was a long silence that stretched out for what seemed like hours as the three exchanged worried looks. Their eyes zapped from each other to me, then back again. The entire display had me crawling out of my skin. I felt as if I had walked into a joke that everyone else was in on except me.

After another few minutes of agony, Rosemary breathed out a long, slow breath. "She'll fit right in."

"Where?" I asked. "Here? With you?"

They didn't have to reply to tell me I was right. *What is happening right now?* Was I being invited to join their bizarre club, and if so, why would I consider it? The last thing I needed was to put more attention on myself and being part of a crime-solving society would not do me any favors. No, what I needed to do was turn around and march out of here immediately. Forget I ever met these people and wipe the entire day from existence.

Go back to my quiet, empty home. Laugh about all of this with Theo.

And yet...

My chin tilted, head lolling backward. I studied the ceiling under the mausoleum, the hair on my arms standing straight. We were directly under the portal here. If something were to happen and the blasted thing was to open, the undertakers would be in serious trouble. Not to mention that I would surely raise suspicion showing up near their hiding place regularly to throw my magic into the doorway. Just because I hadn't seen them before all this didn't mean our paths wouldn't cross again. Especially now that I knew where they spent their time.

The frown lines around my mouth deepened. What to do?

"What do you say, Lyra?" Mortimer asked.

I grimaced. "I'm not sure."

"How about you help us find out what happened to your John Doe and decide after?" Rosemary suggested. "No pressure."

I inspected the watchful gazes of the three before me. Well, two before me. Flinn appeared to want nothing to do with me or the invitation they extended. Still, it was interesting what they were suggesting. And I had to admit, I did desperately want to find John Doe's family. My spine uncurled. I looked at the group, my resolve hardening.

"You know what? Let's do it," I said.

Mortimer and Ellie side glanced each other while

Rosemary came over to shake my hand again. Finn stayed rooted in place, his face unreadable. With every passing second, my stomach churned. Did I make the right decision? Would it come back to haunt me later in life? So many questions swirled in my brain that I couldn't breathe.

Turning away from the group, I raked my gaze over the room and thought about the odd situation I'd landed in. *One step at a time.* And that was the only thing I could do, wasn't it? There was no manual written for joining a secret society of undertakers.

I tapped my chin. Perhaps I could write one.

Chapter Nine

Aside from playing detectives and hiding out in the world's creepiest secret location, the Grim Wardens were actually quite a regular bunch. For undertakers, that was.

After agreeing to join them in their pursuit of the truth for my John Doe, I couldn't wait to get home to tell Theo all about it. If anyone would understand how odd a situation, I'd landed myself in, it would be the cat. On account of his entire life being shaped by an odd, unlikely situation. Unfortunately, the Wardens were not so keen on letting me escape that easily.

Not only did the three ask me to join them for a late lunch—which shockingly got delivered to the cemetery where Ellie picked it up at the gates—but they spent the afternoon chatting about the most mundane things.

We covered everything from Rosemary's knitting to Mortimer's collection of antique cigar cutters. I was even let in on Finn's background, and nothing put me in more unease than knowing that the man that appeared to despise me was ex-military and could likely break me in half if he wished. I glanced at the director of the morgue briefly, finding his gaze turned from me yet again.

What was his problem?

I shook off my aggravation, crammed another bite of pizza in my mouth, and focused on the conversation around the table.

"And that was the final clue we needed to catch the burglar," Mortimer said.

My eyes turned to saucers. "I can't believe you got away with hacking into the bank's security system, Ellie," I said. "That's pretty impressive."

The young undertaker cracked her knuckles with a self-assured grin. "I've been tinkering with computers since I was a kid. It comes naturally now."

"And is a huge asset to the group," Rosemary said. "If there is any dirt you need online, she's the one to get it."

I rubbed my chin. I could think of a few people I wouldn't mind checking up on. Before I could stop it, my gaze landed on Finn again. *Why couldn't I let it go?* I had no idea why it bothered me so much that the man appeared to despise me. Perhaps it was my lack of social skills in this realm, but whatever it was, the mere image of his scowl when he spoke to me made me want to punch things. His perfect nose, in particular.

Peeling my angry eyes off the morgue director, I settled my attention on the rest of the group. It was a strange sensation to be around so many people and not have the urge to run. Usually, when I found myself in a tight space with more than one person, my first reaction was to bury my head in the sand like an ostrich. Elevators were a huge no-no for this reason. And yet, sitting underground with three people I'd met only recently seemed as natural as breathing. Maybe it was because we shared so much in common with our careers that put me at ease.

I twirled the tip of my hair, eyeing the group. "Any guesses on who my John Doe is?"

"Not yet," Rosemary said, her voice soft. "But we'll get there. We always do."

I smiled. "How many cases have you all helped solve over the years?"

"That is an interesting question," Mortimer replied. He pushed his chair back and walked to a nearby shelf to deposit a book he was reading. Running a hand down the shelf, he stopped at one leather spine, pulled it out, and returned to the table. "A lot of the cases we'd helped with only needed minimal discoveries. Because we're civilians, we can go where the police can't, you see. So, we are able to provide them with evidence they otherwise wouldn't have."

"He means local gossip," Finn mumbled.

I laughed. "Does gossip count as evidence these days?"

"Not in the way you're thinking," Mortimer said. "But we are able to get people to talk to us, and talking leads to clues. Those clues can help the police crack a case that otherwise would have run cold. It's a fine line between gossip and knowledge, my dear."

My elbows slid on the oak table as I leaned in. What Mortimer said made sense. Seeing the group gathered under the mausoleum, I could easily see how people would feel comfortable opening up to them. Every single person here had something that made them approachable. Even Finn, who despite his permanent glower, had a face that appeared trustworthy. Plus, who wouldn't trust a mortician with a dirty secret? Whom would they tell?

A phone rang on the opposite side of the room, and I stifled a laugh. The ringtone, a funeral march played at a high-pitched tone, continued until Ellie finally snatched her cellphone from a backpack near the door. She picked it up, walking away from us and disappearing between two bookshelves. The dimness of the space swallowed her entirely; no sound escaping from wher-ever she vanished to.

The grazing of fingers against my arms made me jump, startled.

"Sorry," Rosemary whispered, yanking her hand away. "I didn't mean to scare you."

I pressed my twitching lips into a thin line. "It's all right. I'm usually a little jumpy."

There was a silence that stretched between us as she raked her careful gaze over me, studying my face and expression. For some odd reason, I didn't mind it one bit. Rosemary's demeanor instantly put me at ease. The woman was so calm that she was basically a walking cup of tea and a warm blanket.

Rosemary tapped a long finger on the table between us. "If you ever need someone to talk to, I'm happy to listen."

Wait, what does that mean?

I puffed out my cheeks, biting the inside of one while my nerves skyrocketed. Could she sense my anxiety somehow? I thought I did a good job of hiding it from people, but it's possible I wasn't as great an actress as I assumed. I made a mental note to ask Theo about it later, pushing the thought out of my head for now.

Racking my brain on how to answer, I opened my mouth and was luckily interrupted by the sound of books falling, followed by cursing. My head swiveled to one corner of the room where several large tomes lay crumpled at Finn's feet. His skin flushed, fists forming at his sides.

"Who left all these here?" he bellowed. When no one replied, he looked in the direction Ellie went, his eyes beading. "Figures."

I blew out a low whistle. "What's his deal?" I asked Rosemary.

"Who? Finn?" She cast a glance over her shoulder. "He's a great guy once you get to know him. I know he comes off rough, but he's been through a lot."

"Do you mean his wife dying?"

She nodded. "Amongst other things. As I said, though, Finn's solid. And he's solved more cases than all of us combined, so he's good to have on your side."

I doubted Finn would ever choose a side that included me, but I nodded, anyway. For a while longer, Rosemary and Mortimer told me more tales of their grandeur, each one bringing me joy. It was uncanny how much their little group was able to accomplish. Whatever I may have thought of the Grim Wardens upon first meeting them slowly evaporated, replaced by a sense of pride for the people who cared so deeply for the dead. It was as though the Wardens were able to imbue a final moment of peace to every unresolved case, to each body to grace their funeral homes and morgues, and to leave the world better in the end.

As far as secret societies went, I could do worse than the one I accidentally stumbled on.

Not your society, I remind myself, as Mortimer motioned theatrically before me. *This is not a full-time gig.*

"Pack it up, folks!"

Ellie's shrill voice dragged me from my thoughts and interrupted Mortimer's monologue. The old man seemed offended, but his expression changed quickly when Ellie approached. Her eyes twinkled mischievously, a brown tweed jacket already buttoned up to the collar making her appear more bulky than she was.

In front of me, Rosemary shook her head. "Ellie wins this round," she said. "Get it on the board, Finn!"

My brows furrowed as I watched Finn wrestle a whiteboard on wheels into the room. The casters squeaked against the floor, but he seemed unbothered, determined as ever. He paused once he had the board positioned to his liking, then reached into the small plastic compartment attached to the frame and pulled out a black marker. Without a word, he uncapped it and leaned in to add another bold stroke under Ellie's name, the fresh ink standing out against the grid of tally marks that filled the board.

Curiosity pulled my gaze downward, and I started counting the lines. Each member of the group had their own column, marked by neat rows of hash marks. Ellie had seven, and others hovered around a similar number. My eyes shifted to the far-right column, where Finn's name was etched. His tally stretched like a mountain, the final count towering above the rest at fifteen. My chest tightened, and I grimaced. Fifteen notches. What kind of game was Finn winning—and at whose expense?

I pointed to the board. "What's this about?"

"First clue point board," Rosemary replied. "Every time one of us gets the first clue to a case, they get a marker. Winner for the month gets a free dinner of their choice. It keeps us motivated."

"But how do you know Ellie found one?"

I turned to look at the youngest member of the group, but she was already out the door.

"Trust me," Rosemary said, patting my hand. "She did. Let's see what it is."

We were about to stand up when Ellie's head popped through the doorway. Her eyebrows wiggled as she checked the whiteboard, stance relaxing. "Checking you're not cheating me out of a steak," she said. Then, looking at me, added, "Your guy was seen arguing with someone at the diner."

"Wow! You're good," I said.

Ellie's grin grew a few inches. "I know. What are you waiting for? Let's go, everyone!"

In a flash, she was gone, leaving us standing around

the library with our jaws agape. I took my time moving and gave the others a chance to get dressed, since I never bothered to take my coat off. As they shrugged on their layers, my stomach tightened, and my temples throbbed. The group was...efficient. Less than a day had passed, and they already had more than I was able to gather on my own.

A tight lump formed in my throat. It was going to be a shame to leave the Grim Wardens behind, once we figured who John Doe was.

"You coming?"

I blinked rapidly, looking up at Finn hovering beside me. He held the large metal door, waiting for me to slip past. Forcing a wooden grin, I squared my shoulders and marched toward him. "I wouldn't miss it for the world."

Chapter Ten

There was something about walking into a small-town diner with four undertakers in tow that really set the vibe for the day. I jiggled the loose handle of the Coral Reef Diner, shoving the door open. Above my head, the welcome bell rang out, but no one inside appeared to notice our presence. As was common for the quaint restaurant, it was packed with more patrons than staff. The Wardens pushed in behind me one by one, until we crowded the space in the front of the diner like clowns in a circus car. My gaze traveled up and down the dimly lit space, and my stomach churned at the smell of burnt oil filling the air.

Inside, the once-red vinyl booths were worn and cracked, with duct tape patching the most well-used seats. The linoleum floor, yellowed and scuffed, gave a sticky sensation with each step, and the faint smell of bleach made my stomach churn with each step. Near to us, a server wiped down the chipped Formica surface of a table, her disinterested expression a mirror to everyone else in the space. The windows of the diner were streaked with fingerprints, and the view of the parking lot outside was blurred by years of grime.

Yet despite its shabby appearance, there was a strange charm to the place—Coral Reef was the kind of diner where secrets were exchanged over weak coffee. I hoped today might be a day some of those will spill out and lend us a hand in getting answers.

A woman in her late fifties walked past us, her apron strings floating behind her as she wiggled into the cramped space behind the hostess stand. She smiled without making eye contact with anyone in our group. "Table for five?" she asked. "Lunch or dinner?"

I glanced at my watch. It was only three o'clock in the afternoon, but I supposed that was prime dinner time for some people. In my periphery, a server balanced a plate of pot pie slathered with gravy on his right arm, his left holding onto a tray of drinks. He expertly averted a kid running through the aisles before dropping off the order at a table occupied by three elderly ladies. They thanked him vigorously, one lady batting her lashes at the server in a way that made me very uncomfortable.

Coral Reef tended to bring in an interesting blend of patrons. It was the type of place you either loved or hated. The food was often burnt, but the prices were right, and the atmosphere was less pretentious than the bougie restaurant on the cliffs.

"Lunch or dinner?" the hostess repeated.

"Drinks, actually," Finn said over my shoulder. "If that's all right."

Judging by the glower on the woman's face, it was most definitely not all right. Her jaw tensed as she picked up a stack of menus and led us to an empty table at the back of the diner. We were right across from the bathroom and wedged between two stands the servers used to dump dishes on.

I nudged Rosemary's side. "I guess most people come here to eat," I said, sliding into a chair. It rattled under my weight, one of the legs shorter than the other three.

A loud banging sound came from the kitchen not far from us, followed by a man cursing loudly.

Rosemary's mouth twisted.

"I think I'll settle for a coffee," she said, sidling next to me. "Suddenly, I'm not too hungry."

A pile of laminated sheets dropped on the table in front of us with a dull thud. "Menus," the hostess said blandly. "In case you change your mind. Someone will be by to take your order shortly."

She left without another word, leaving us with stained menus and not a drink in sight.

"Friendly place," Finn said.

Mortimer chuckled under his breath. He reached a pockmarked hand over the table and snatched a menu, perusing it with little interest. "It certainly seems to be for a specific taste."

"Or no taste," Ellie remarked. "As in, no taste buds."

Everyone took a menu, and we spent the next few minutes painstakingly reading through the options. Each selection was more grease-covered than the next, and I briefly wondered how anyone walked out with anything but clogged arteries when they left this place. Looking around, though, it didn't seem to bother the patrons filling the diner to the brim. If anything, it was likely what drew the crowd in. In an era when everyone was concerned about their health, the Coral Reef boasted the opposite. "Come on in!" it seemed to shout. "Live a little."

I watched a man devour fries drenched in gravy at the table across from us. The menu dropped from my hands, and I shoved it away, ordering a simple sparkling water when the server finally showed up to take our order. Much like the hostess, he left with a scowl on his face after he jotted down the drinks we requested.

My gaze darted around the diner before landing on Ellie. "I can't picture John Doe in this place."

"Why not?" Finn asked.

"When I examined the body, he struck me as someone who had the means to dine in much better restaurants."

Finn raised a bushy brow my way. "In other words, he was filthy rich."

"I mean, I can't say for certain," I retracted. "But if I had to guess, I'd wager he was, yes."

Finn swirled in the chair so he could face Ellie, fixing her with the same serious glare he seemed to be born with. "What's your source again?"

The young woman didn't reply at first, her silence stretching into something almost uncomfortable. Instead, she glanced down at her watch, a sleek silver piece that glinted under the blunt fluorescent diner lights. Her pointed nose wrinkled ever so slightly, as though the act of waiting offended her. The sound of her nails tapping a restless rhythm against the Formica tabletop filled the space between us.

Her leg, pressed against mine beneath the narrow booth, bounced with a nervous energy, transmitting her tension through every jitter. When her neck craned forward, stretching as she leaned toward the aisle, I caught a glimpse of anticipation in her expression. Whatever she was looking for, it was clear she'd found it.

Ellie's lips curled upward into a knowing grin.

"There she is," she said.

All four of us turned to see who she meant. My eyes bulged as a long-legged, stunning woman approached our table. She wore the same apron the hostess and server had on—the diner's uniform—and yet on her it appeared almost regal. And that was despite the oil stains on the front.

The woman tightened her thick chocolate-brown ponytail as she approached. She had a face made for modeling, all angles, and a body that I only saw on famous people in movies. To sum up, she was the sort of attractive that left you speechless, no matter who you were.

My eyes flashed to Finn and a sordid part of me was relieved when I didn't find him drooling. I shook the thought away before it could take root in my brain and concentrated on the goddess hovering over our table.

"Ellie, darling, hello again," she said, her voice soft as butter. "When I said come by, I didn't realize you'd be here instantly."

Ellie chuckled. "You know me, Margie. Always the over-achiever. Now, what can you tell me about the man you mentioned on the phone?"

"The rich guy or the other one?"

"Either," Mortimer replied.

At this, Margie folded her arms over her large chest

and sucked in a slow breath. Her apron struggled under the pressure of the motion as though it might tear any second. When she breathed out, I relaxed with the polyester fabric.

"I can't tell you much about the suit," she replied. "But the one he argued with will be easy." She gestured to a table near a window with her chin. "He's right over there."

Chairs scraped over the sticky linoleum floor as we all turned in unison. Ellie and Rosemary lifted off their seats to see the man better, while Finn and Mortimer ground their teeth loud enough for others to overhear. I pressed my elbows into the table and arched my back to inspect our first suspect. *Um. Not suspect.* A bystander who knew John Doe and may or may not have been responsible for his doubtfully natural death. Whatever the term was for the man, he was definitely an interesting character.

With hair covered in enough gel to render it entirely stiff, a crooked nose, and green eyes so beady they belonged in the skull of a rat, the man was nothing short of suspicious. He had the look of someone you couldn't trust—a person you would cross the street to avoid. Before him lay an open manila file folder, and he perused its contents with the precision of a sharpened steak knife. All this to say that I didn't trust this stranger to tell the truth. Not one bit.

"I don't like him," Finn announced shortly.

My jaw clenched. "Neither do I," I agreed. "What's our plan?"

No one spoke. For all their secrecy and heroic stories, the Wardens were very ill prepared for this moment. My face scrunched up as I waited for someone to make a move. When it appeared that no one would, I rolled my eyes and stood up.

"Where are you going?" Mortimer asked.

I pointed to the man's table. "To talk to him," I answered. "Isn't that what we came here to do?"

"Oh. We usually take things a tad slower, dear," Mortimer said. "We observe, we report. We wait."

That was not going to work for me. Not only did I not have time to waste, but the idea of staying in the dive diner a minute longer had me crawling out of my skin. Not to mention all the people around. I was already dreaming of coming home to shut the door behind me, and it wasn't even two in the afternoon yet. Not to mention the work I had lined up for the day and the preparations for this weekend's visitation.

I would be way behind schedule if I followed the Wardens' lead. Before anyone could object further, I down the rest of my water to clear my dry throat, turned on my heel, and stomped toward the man. A second later, a second set of footsteps joined mine as Finn hurried to flank my side.

I glanced at him out of the corner of my eye. "What happened to observing and reporting?"

The tall morgue director grinned. "Can't let you have all the fun," he said. "So, what's our cover story?"

We reached the table faster than anticipated. Finn hadn't even finished speaking when we found ourselves bumping against the booth with the man in question staring up at us in confusion. I glimpsed down at the open folder on the table, brow creasing. The folder was full of real estate listings. I recognized some of the pictures as recent homes up for sale in Orchard Hollow, all located in the more expensive areas of town.

The man caught me staring and closed the folder quickly.

"Can I help you?" he asked.

"Hi, there," Finn said. "We're sorry to interrupt."

He was about to continue, but for some Fairy-saken reason, I opened my mouth instead. "Whom were you arguing with in this diner three days ago?" I blurted out.

Both Finn and the man raised an eyebrow at me.

"Sorry," I said quickly. "My name is Lyra Moore. I am the funeral director over at Mistbrook Manor."

The man frowned. "I don't think I follow."

"There was a man you argued with at this very diner," I tried to explain. "That man is now in my morgue. That is to say, he died. And you may have been the last person to have seen him alive."

The man paused for a long while. His eyes glazed over like he was trying to put together a puzzle with missing pieces. Thin lips puckering, he worried his hands on the table, sending the folder sliding across the shiny surface.

"That doesn't make any sense," he said softly. "The only person I met in town is... Wait, are you telling me Charles is dead?"

A jolt ripped at my heart. I looked at Finn, whose expression was a mirror of mine. We had a name! The body I received was not a John Doe anymore; he was Charles. I bit the inside of my cheek. *Charles, what?*

My focus landed on the man in the booth.

"We're sorry to be the ones to deliver the news," Finn said. "Was Charles the one you fought with then? And sorry, I didn't catch your name."

Smooth move. I snuck a glance at Finn. *Color me impressed, sir.*

"It's Arthur," the man at the booth said. "Arthur Malone. And I truly wouldn't call my conversation with Charles a fight."

I grimaced. "One of the servers mentioned that it was quite a heated conversation."

Arthur barked out a laugh. "If you knew Charles, you'd know every conversation with him was heated. But no, we did not fight that day." He patted the file folder in front of him. "I'm a real estate agent, you see.

The Whitmores are long-time clients of mine. I'm their agent for high-end listings in Orchard Hollow."

"Whitmore..." Finn whispered. "Sounds familiar."

"It should! Charles and his family own half of King City. His grandfather was a big player in the oil business," Arthur said. "And Charles is—" His eyes wetted, and he swiped at them with the sleeve of his suit. "—*was* a brilliant developer. He was here scoping out a few locations for his next venture and wanted me to put in a bid on a place I didn't think he should consider."

Finn's shoulders stiffened. He rolled his neck, his vision lasering in on the real estate agent. "Why not?"

"Too messy," Arthur replied. "The owner was attached to the place. It would have cost Charles too much to buy them out. Not worth it, in my opinion. Which is what I told him. Thus, the argument."

"Did Charles spend a lot of time in Orchard Hollow?" I asked.

Arthur shook his head. "Not at all," he said. "We usually did all our business on the phone."

"Why the trip out this time?"

"You know, I'm not sure. He must have needed to get away," Arthur said. "The city can be hectic."

His face darkened as though he had the same thought as me. It's possible that if Charles stayed in the city, he would still be alive. So far, we didn't have anything to imply that his death was not accidental, and

I was beginning to believe that I made the entire thing up in my head. But then how would that explain the tox report? And why *did* Charles come out here now, of all times?

We seemed to have more questions than answers.

The pit in my stomach shriveled slightly. We had a name. That was more than we walked in with. First, we needed to verify we had the right guy, and sadly, to break the news to Arthur. I pulled out my phone, my hand shaking slightly as I pulled up the photo I took of John Doe. Slowly, I inched the screen toward Arthur. "I'm sorry to have to do this, but can you confirm that this is, in fact, Charles Whitmore?"

Arhtur's face blanched. He sucked in a sharp breath and closed his eyes tightly, nodding. After a few more unsteady breaths, he opened his eyes again to look at me.

"When will you be releasing the body?"

My head spun around to Arthur, eyes rounding. "Pardon me?"

"Charles," he said. "His mother will want to bury him in the family plot. I assume that now that he's no longer a John Doe, arrangements will be made for a transfer to the city."

I nodded. "There will be, yes. We'll make sure to let the police know and have someone contact Mrs. Whitmore. Would you mind giving me her number? I'd like to send my condolences."

Without a second thought, Arthur scribbled a number on a piece of paper and handed it to me. I folded it up, tucking it into my purse for safekeeping as he said, "That's her personal line. She doesn't give it out, but I'm sure in this case it's fine." He breathed out slowly. "I can't believe he's gone."

"I'm really sorry for your loss," I said softly.

"Me too," Finn agreed. "If you can think of anything else we should tell the police, here's my card."

The phone on the table rang and Arthur looked at the screen, quickly pressing it to his ear. "I have to take this, I'm afraid," he said. "Family matters."

Thanking Arthur for the help he provided, we turned around and walked back to the table of three very eager-looking Wardens. They spoke over one another, asking questions about what we found out. While Finn filled them in, I stared out the window, my chest rising and falling with a definitive calm. We figured it out. Charles Whitmore was going to get a proper burial, and he had the Grim Wardens to thank for it.

Mortimer was not kidding around; they really were good at this sort of thing.

Chapter Eleven

"You are an abomination upon fairy kind," Theo drawled. "An absolute embarrassment."

My hands dropped away from the rosebush and a growl formed in my chest. I looked at the cat, frustration rising deep within me. "Can you please give me a moment of peace for once?"

Gray fur rippled as Theo stretched out on his tippy toes. His spine curved and his tail shot straight up into the air. He ran his talons on the wooden bench, catching the grain with a satisfactory grin on his whiskered face.

"Must I be the only voice of reason in this deranged household?" he asked. "You have discovered a secret society and instead of rushing in to fill your life with intrigue and excitement, you've been over here chopping up plants. Appalling, truly."

I groaned. "I am not chopping anything," I announced. I wiped the dirt from my hands on my pants. "The roses must be trimmed to survive the winter. And I have no reason to involve myself with the Grim Wardens. If you missed the most integral part of the story, we know who Charles is now. His family can bury the man, and the police can close the case. End of story."

"A very boring and uneventful story, I say."

For the rest of the afternoon, I chose to ignore the cat and concentrate on tending to the garden and the elated feeling in my chest. The Wardens came through big time. I didn't know how far I would have gotten without their help in identifying Charles Whitmore, but I certainly knew it wouldn't have happened in the span of a lunchtime. The tip from the server was a blessing, one I wasn't taking lightly.

For once, I didn't completely hate getting roped into socializing.

I looked at the roses blooming before me. "Maybe I should send them a thank you bouquet."

"You want to send a flower arrangement to the undertakers?" Theo asked incredulously. "The people who have to deal with the dreadful things for their work."

I swallowed hard. "You're right. It would be odd."

"It would be desperate," the cat corrected. "Which is right on brand for you, so go for it."

I pulled off my gardening gloves, balled them up, and tossed them at the cat. They missed by a foot. The gloves ricocheted off the back of the bench and came catapulting back at me, smacking me in the shoulder as though to mock my attempt at violence.

Theo's cackling laugh echoed past me.

I rolled my eyes. "If I were Bartholomew, I'd have sent you through as a worm."

The cat's mouth opened to retort with a witty comeback, but he was interrupted by the doorbell. I arched my back, peeking around the rosebush to see who it might be. From this side of the manor, I could catch a glimpse of the front porch well enough to make out the shape of a short woman with hair whiter than fresh-fallen snow. She wore a pair of gold-rimmed glasses fastened around her neck with a silver chain. The coat she wore was a brown tweed that reminded me of clothing a grandmother might wear; it was quite functional and not at all stylish. Which made sense, because if I had to guess, I'd put the woman somewhere in her late seventies.

The most important part of her appearance wasn't what she wore, though. It was that I had no idea who she was.

I exchanged twin looks of worry with Theo before standing up and skirting around the house to greet the stranger. As I approached, more of the woman came into my view and I instantly regretted not pretending to be away. The 'Do Not Disturb' sign was still facing out on the door; I could have easily stayed out of this.

The woman, oblivious to me standing at the base of the stairs behind her, pressed her nose to the glass of my bay window. Her hands formed walls on either side of her face as she continued to spy on my home. Her breath fogged up the glass. It would surely need a good cleaning after she left.

The muscle in my jaw feathered.

I cleared my throat, making the woman jump away from the window.

"Hello," I said. "May I help you?"

The woman's eyes widened, and the thickness of her glasses made them look even bigger. She looked to be imitating an owl caught in headlights. Tucking a strand of white hair behind her ear, she touched the tip of her pointed chin, saying, "Good afternoon. Is the funeral director around to speak to?"

"You're looking at her," I replied.

The woman raked her green eyes over the dirt stains on my pants, her gaze freezing on my nails blackened by the earth from the garden.

"I was out back gardening," I said, the excuse tasting

sour on my tongue. "But I assure you, you have the right person. What can I do for you?"

"Oh," the woman said. The words sounded like a sigh. She extended her hand to me, and I shook it reluctantly. "Maggie Halloway."

I crossed my arms over my chest and nodded. "Lyra Moore. Welcome to Mistbrook Funeral Home, Maggie. I hope this isn't an unpleasant visit."

It took the woman a second to catch on, and when she did, her brows shot up into her hairline. "Oh! You mean... No, nothing of the sort. I'm a librarian at the Orchard Hollow library."

I wasn't sure what her profession was supposed to imply in this particular situation.

When I didn't say anything in return, Maggie frowned, continuing. "I wanted to ask you about one of your—" She paused, "—patients? Is that the right word?"

"Do you mean one of the deceased?"

Maggie nodded eagerly. "Yes, that's it. A deceased by the name of Charles Whitmore."

Hmm. Why did a librarian need to know anything about a rich guy from the city? It was strange enough she showed up here, but to come asking questions about a peculiar case was suspicious at best. Unless she was another Grim Warden that the group forgot to mention?

I shook my head. That couldn't possibly be it. For one, she wasn't an undertaker. And if she needed information on Charles, she could have gotten it from the other members of the secret society.

Everything about this screamed wrong to me.

"Are you a family member?" I asked, trying to keep the doubt from my voice.

The librarian bristled. "No, I've never met the man," she replied. "Was it a natural death? Did you find any signs of foul play? What did the police have to say? Or have they not been involved?"

The woman fired off questions like she was working a machine gun. I stumbled back, my butt colliding with one of the planters flanking the stairs. The roses shivered from the impact, and I felt myself shiver with them. Why did Maggie need to know all these things?

"I'm sorry, I'm not sure I follow," I said. "If you're not related to Mr. Whitmore, why do you need this information?"

My comment appeared to have knocked some sense into her because she blinked rapidly, her bulging frames sliding down the ridge of her nose. Maggie tucked them back into place with a single forefinger, her lips pressing tightly together.

She shimmied her angular shoulders. "I have a professional interest in the case."

"For the library?"

"In a way," Maggie answered.

The cryptic nature of her reply made Finn come to

mind. I immediately pushed the image of him out of my head, since the mere thought of the morgue director made me uneasy. Instead, I focused on the possible threat standing across from me. All one hundred-and-ten-ish pounds of her.

"I'm sorry to disappoint," I said sternly, "but I'm afraid I cannot divulge any information to anyone that is not family."

"Right, of course. I understand."

The dissatisfaction in Maggie's tone showed that she did not understand at all and was, in fact, quite upset that I didn't give her anything of value.

"Well, if you change your mind, you know where to find me. Thanks for your time." She brushed past me, stomping her purple boots down the steps. On the way out, she eyed the roses I stood next to, turning to look at me over her shoulder. "If you're in need of a florist, Daisy Rivers has a great little shop on Dandelion Avenue. She's fairly new here, but the shop has a lovely selection, and her cousin has been in Orchard Hollow for ages, so she's stuck with us now. Tell her Maggie sent you when you visit."

With that, she swirled on her heel and marched to the banana-yellow sedan parked behind my truck. As the librarian sped away, I couldn't stop the exasperation from drowning out every other thought but the last ten minutes.

My gaze landed on the roses.

"Don't worry," I told the flowers. "She wouldn't know a proper rose if it smacked her in her spectacles."

Groaning, I made sure Maggie was long gone before opening the front door and shutting it tightly behind me. The definitive clicks of the locks made my posture slump in relief. As I made my way to the kitchen for a much-needed pot of tea, I couldn't help but replay what happened. It wasn't the librarian that bothered me, though she was plenty bothersome. Her presence here made me realize an oddly important thing.

Could it be possible that Charles Whitmore's case wasn't as open-and-shut as I thought? And if it wasn't, what were I and the other undertakers missing?

Chapter Twelve

The Orchard Hollow library was nestled on a wide residential street not far from the main beach entrance. It was an adorable, ivy-covered brick building that dated back over a century; at least, that was what the bronze sign on the wall read. The building was quite small for a library, perhaps even smaller than the one the Wardens used for their hide-away, but it made up for its lack in size with character and charm. Large arched windows sat on either side of a deep-green door, and light poured in through them and frosted over the polished hardwood floors. To the right of the front door, an antique wood desk sat under a vintage chandelier, the light bouncing around the wall-to-wall bookshelves as it swayed lightly.

The air in the library smelled of old books, and I

sensed a hint of lavender that came and went now and again.

I stood behind the spiral staircase in the back that led to a loft area with more books arranged on tall shelves. From here, I had a perfect view of the front desk, where I assumed Maggie Halloway would sit had she been in today. Instead, the chair was occupied by a young man with a flair for fashion and a lack of care for much of anything else in the library.

There were a few people lingering about the space. A man worked on his laptop at a desk at the rear, positioned near the large windows overlooking the playground across the street. Two moms chatted in the kids' area while their toddlers ran havoc through the aisles. And a group of teens gathered around the plush armchairs in one corner, each holding a book they weren't actually reading.

My fingers wrapped tightly over the spine of the random book I picked up. I pressed my shoulders into the wood railing of the stairs, my mood deflating. What was I even doing here? Stalking the librarian was not on my to-do list for the day.

Resolving to leave, I pushed away from the stairs and started for the exit. My feet froze in place. Eyes rounding, I watched as the front door burst open and a familiar face poked inside. Finn O'Malley walked through the library like a man on a mission. His long legs glided across the hardwood floors, and I tried not to flinch at the ripple of muscle under his annoyingly tight sweater. My gaze scanned the surroundings for a place to get out of his sightline, but there was no use.

Finn was already heading directly for me.

As he approached, I shrank into the shadows in the hope that I could disappear within them. If there was ever a time to want to open another portal, this was it. Bad enough I was wasting my time stalking a librarian, but now I had a witness to my nosiness.

I coughed into the sleeve of my jacket as Finn's form grew larger before me.

"Lyra," he said, inching closer. "Funny running into you here."

I cringed. "Yes, small world. Checking out a book?"

There was a gap in conversation as Finn regarded me. His expression was that of someone trying to decide if they can trust a person or throw them across the room. If I didn't have so many of my own secrets, I'd have been offended.

Finally, Finn's brow twitched, and he leaned in closer, his voice a whisper when he said, "If I tell you something, do you promise to keep it to yourself?"

A lump formed in my throat. I swallowed it down, nodding.

"I'm looking into a suspicion I have about the last case the Wardens took on."

The lump returned.

"Charles Whitmore?" I asked.

"Correct."

My shoulders hiked up high enough to graze my earlobes. "I thought that was a shut case. We have his name, and the family has been notified."

"This case isn't sitting right with me," Finn admitted. "Thought I'd see what else I can find out about the guy and why he was here in town. But I didn't want to waste the others' time unless I had a reason to."

I smirked tightly. "Thus, the secrecy."

"Bingo," Finn said. "What brings you to the library?"

My lips downturned as the smile melted away into a frown. I could very well lie. It was simple enough to make up a story and leave Finn behind, never to speak to him or the other undertakers ever again. But why would I? He was here for the same reason I was. No matter how much I tried to stay out of it, Charles Whitmore remained on my mind. There had to be a reason for that. One that I wouldn't mind figuring out.

I wanted the truth more than I wanted to get away from Finn. A first.

"Honestly, I'm here because of Charles too," I admitted.

The morgue director's jaw tensed, making it appear

that much sharper. "You also think his death is suspicious?"

"I wouldn't go that far. But someone came around today asking too many questions, and it raised some questions." I pointed to the checkout counter. "I was hoping to run into the librarian here to see why she wanted to know the details about Charles. It was odd."

To my utter surprise, Finn chuckled.

"You mean Maggie?" he asked.

"You know her?"

Another laugh, this one low and warm. "Everyone who works with dead people knows Maggie Halloway. She's writing a true crime book about Orchard Hollow. If someone dies, Maggie would be all over that." He crooked an eyebrow at me. "I'm surprised she hasn't harassed you before."

My spine curled in on itself. "She hasn't," I said, unable to hide the disappointment in my voice. "I guess I was exaggerating."

"Ha! Mortimer would be the first to tell that exaggeration is a sign of a true truth seeker."

"Mortimer would be giving me too much credit."

Eyes darkening, Finn gaped at me down the length of his nose. His chest rose and fell with heavy breaths, and I suddenly felt way too exposed. As though I woke up in one of those dreams where you're on stage in front of an audience in your underwear. It was unnerving the way this man could make me feel so small and so big all at the same time.

I could see how that would be a handy skill in his extracurricular activities. No wonder Finn closed more cases than anyone else in the group—who could withstand this level of complete intimidation?

"Since you're already here," he said. "How do you feel about teaming up?"

My bones shivered. "I beg your pardon?"

"Two heads are better than one," Finn continued. "And I could use a second pair of eyes. I don't know if you've seen the town's records—" He pointed to the loft area above our heads, "—but it's a mess up there. I could certainly use the assist. Unless you have other plans already."

An image of Theo complaining about my movie choices flashed before my eyes. I sighed. "No other plans," I said softly. "Lead the way."

Finn took the lead, and I trailed behind him up the spiral steps and onto the upper level of the library. The view from up here was a lovely sight, with rows of bookshelves dividing the space below like trails in a forest. I noticed the teenagers had made a home at one of the long communal desks, and my heart warmed to see their stacks of books. In an era when everyone was attached to their tech gadgets, it was nice to see that kids still enjoyed reading.

I spun around to find Finn settling in at a chair opposite a row of computers. We, on the other hand...we were all about the tech today, it seemed.

"Where do you usually start?" I asked Finn. "When you're working a case, that is."

He turned on a computer, sliding his chair in. "It depends. Now that we have a name, I would likely do a broad search. Check social media profiles, see if there are any hits on articles."

"If the Whitmores were as important as Arthur led us to believe, there'd be a lot to sift through," I mused. My eyes narrowed. "That's what I'm here for, I take it?"

"If you don't mind."

I pulled out the chair next to him. "Not at all. Why don't you check the social sites, and I'll see what I can find out about the family?" I suggested.

When Finn agreed to the plan, I sank into the chair, which was quite comfortable and full of bounce, and got to work. I was relieved he didn't put me in charge of scouring Charles Whitmore's social media. The thought of sifting through selfies for the next who-knew-how-long was more excruciating than listening to Theo recount his tales of Fairy.

Cracking my knuckles, I ignored the grimace the sound earned me from Finn and got to work.

After almost an hour of searching, we were nowhere closer to unraveling the mirage that was Charles Whitmore. Finn found a few profiles registered to the man, but they were fairly empty, with only a few photos of lunches and one detailed post about a cottage trip. The rest of the hits were all business-related, and recounted multiple deals the Whitmores made in the last decade. It appeared the real estate agent was not painting a false picture. The family was slowly taking over King City with how many buildings and construction sites they purchased.

I wondered what anyone would want with that much land. I supposed I wasn't the right person to judge, though. I couldn't even fathom living in the city, let alone in a skyscraper, which, as it turned out, was most of the purchases.

A thought occurred to me as I studied the blueprints of a current project Whitmore Industries was producing. I turned in the seat to face Finn. "Hey, didn't Arthur say that he was trying to talk Charles out of buying a building here in town?"

"He did, yes," Finn answered. "What are you thinking?"

"I'm not too sure yet. Give me a second."

Typing in several search phrases into the top bar, I pulled up a few articles and scanned them. As I continued to scroll through the results, one article stood from a small online paper a few towns over. I clicked on it, my pulse thrumming faster.

"Check this out," I told Finn. *"King City Real Estate Mogul Devouring Orchard Hollow. Is Stanton Next?"*

Finn leaned over my shoulder to look at the screen. The woodsy smell of his cologne penetrated my nostrils. My nose itched instantly.

"Bold headline," Finn said, continuing to read. "This says Charles was after the Whistling Kettle."

I arched my brow. "The tea shop on Cliff Row?"

When Finn nodded, I noticed the same excitement I felt, mirrored in his expression. My chest heaved with a sharp breath that I held in for way longer than was necessary. Blowing it out, I glanced at Finn, my teeth splitting into a grin. "Are you thinking what I'm thinking?" I asked.

Finn returned my smile. "I wouldn't mind a cup of tea right about now. Let's go."

As he turned off our respective computers and pulled out my chair, I tried to focus on the tea shop and not the way my heart pitter-pattered a little too fast. Finn was only being nice because we had a lead. He was a distraction I couldn't afford right now. Besides, there was no fairy way I would ever date an undertaker. I had enough death of my own to deal with.

Chapter Thirteen

The Whistling Kettle was quite possibly the cutest business on Cliff Row. Tucked between a bookstore—Brooks Books—and a yarn supply shop, the local tea spot was all softness and charm. Its exterior, painted a pastel yellow, had white-trimmed windows, and flower boxes that were decorated with colorful gnomes and holiday ornaments. I secretly wished to sneak over after dark and bloom some florals for the display, but that would draw too much attention.

With Finn padding softly behind me, I raked my gaze over the wooden sign hanging above the door. The name of the shop had begun to fade, but the swirly letters were still visible enough that you couldn't miss the place if you tried.

With a nod at Finn, I pulled the door open, smiling

at the ding-dong of the overhead bell. Inside, the shop was so warm I had to take my coat off immediately. The aroma of different teas filled the shop; my stomach grumbled when I noted the scent of freshly baked scones mixed in.

Shelves lined with jars of loose-leaf tea, labeled in handwritten script, crowded the walls on either side of us. Between them, mismatched furniture of wooden tables and floral-patterned chairs battled for floor real estate. My chest tickled when I spotted the small fireplace in the far corner of the shop.

That explains the heat.

Not far from it stood a display counter with an antique cash register sitting atop it. My eyes narrowed on the sweet, blue-haired lady behind the counter. The owner of the Whistling Kettle wore a floral apron that oddly matched the chairs we passed, and she watched us while cashing out another customer. Her unrelenting, sharp gaze rolled over me, then proceeded to inspect Finn. If I had to guess, I'd say she was making notes on every detail of our appearance, from our heads to our toes.

The woman handed a yellow paper bag to the customer, tied with a matching lace ribbon. "Here you go, love," she said. "Make sure you come back to try the lavender lemon we have coming in next month!"

"Will do, Mrs. Dawson," the woman said.

The customer brushed past us, carrying the smell of her tea leaves out the door. As the door swung closed and the bell rang out, a boisterous laugh rose from one of the tables where a couple sipped from two large mugs. They clinked their glasses together, the steam of the tea rising between them.

My belly twisted. We were definitely interrupting their date. Maybe this was the wrong time to visit.

Before I could tell Finn I changed my mind, the morgue director skirted around me and took one long stride toward the counter and the woman behind it.

"Afternoon," he said, his hand outstretched.

The woman shook it vehemently. Then giggled like a schoolgirl. "Welcome to the Whistling Kettle, love," she said. "I'm Edith Dawson. Can I interest you in a sample of our Orchid Chai tea today?"

"Thank you, Edith," Finn replied. "That sounds lovely. I take it you're the proud owner of this absolutely marvelous establishment?"

The sparkle in Finn's eyes made me suppress a laugh. He was laying the charm on thick. Who was this guy? Surely not the somber man I knew. I chuckled into the sleeve of my coat.

"I certainly am, young man," Edith cooed.

Edith's eyes flared, making my heart drop into my boots. Clearing my throat of the multiple knots forming there, I stepped forward. I supposed it would be decisively odd if I let Finn do all the talking. Luckily, I loved a good cup of tea, so it wouldn't be too hard to convince the woman we were here for honest reasons.

I looked at the display on the counter, picking out a small tin. "You have a marvelous selection," I told the shop owner.

"Always lovely to meet another tea lover," Edith said. She pointed to the tin I held. "Wonderful selection. The Double Cream Earl Gray is our most popular choice. Should I put on a pot for you two?"

"We won't be staying long," Finn said, at the same time as I uttered, "Yes, please."

We exchanged frustrated glances.

The shop owner clocked them instantly, smiling. "Couples these days," she muttered.

I started to tell her that Finn and I were quite far from being a couple, but the woman cut me off before I could say a word. She nodded to the couple at the window table. "Now you see those two there? They've been coming here for three years, been together as long," she said. "And he is yet to propose. Marta's sister says Marta is not too pleased about it either."

An elbow nudged into my side. I turned slightly toward Finn, who had his eyebrows raised at the shop owner. It appeared Edith was a bit of a gossip. I grinned. *Excellent.*

Oblivious to our expressions of pure glee, Edith

turned to the burner behind her. She dropped several loose leaves of tea into a pot, then set it on the burner, adjusting the temperature before facing us again. Her eyes crinkled at the edges.

"The Earl Gray will be ready shortly," she announced. "Why don't you two take a seat for now? I'll get you a few scones while you wait. Freshly baked from this morning!"

My mouth salivated at the mention of food. So when Finn opened *his* mouth to object, I grabbed his arm and pulled him after me, marching to a table near the wall. The white lace tablecloth brushed against my thighs as I squeezed in, and I had to press my palms on the table to keep the dreaded thing from sliding right off and taking the vase of pansies along with it. The vase wobbled, but straightened out without incident.

I breathed out in relief.

Looking up, I noticed Finn watching me intently, his expression, as always, unreadable. I bit the inside of my cheek before asking, "What?"

"Nothing. Are you always this clumsy?"

My skin flushed. "Are you always this rude?"

"Fair point," Finn said. His lips edged into a smile. He fought it tooth and nail. "Edith seems like a chatterbox. I think we can probably get her to talk about the sale of this place if we play our cards right."

Glancing over my shoulder, I watched the tea shop

owner busy herself with our tray while keeping one eye on the couple by the window. They were deep in conversation and judging by the way the woman's hands flayed around, it wasn't a pleasant one. Edith's ears lengthened and her entire body shifted forward to hear better.

Could she be any more obvious?

I rolled my eyes, turning to Finn. "You're probably right. How did you get so good at this, anyway?"

"You mean the stuff with society?" Finn asked. "I always had an eye for details. It's how I got to where I am with the hospital. But it was Jenny that made me realize there was more to my work than paperwork. She believed in the Wardens and all they represented, thought it was a valiant path."

I cocked my head sideways. "She sounds like she was a wonderful person."

"She was," Finn replied.

"I know I said it before, but I'm very sorry for your loss," I said. "Losing someone you love is never easy."

Finn's face darkened, a storm forming behind his eyes. "Has someone in your life died?"

My body grew rigid, and my hands fisted. I shoved them under the table, hiding the anxiety that rose to the surface from plain sight. My heart thundered.

I fought against the bile rolling up into my throat, a

feeling I was used to when I thought about Fairy. Glancing at Finn, I looked away immediately.

"Not exactly," I said. "But my family... It's complicated."

Across from me, Finn appeared as if he was about to say something but was interrupted by the clinking of glasses approaching our table. Edith floated over to us, a tray of dainty cups and a steaming teapot balanced in her hands. Between the cups sat two small plates, each one holding fluffy raspberry scones glazed with honey.

I wiped the saliva drooping from the side of my mouth as the shop owner put the tray down and slid it to the center of the table.

She poured tea into each of the cups and sat them in front of us. "Enjoy!" she said brightly.

"Thank you, Edith," Finn said. Picking up his cup, he sniffed the air and sat it down again. The steam from the cup bounced off the visor of his newsboy cap, fogging up his face momentarily. When the air cleared, his eyes were focused on the shop owner. "It smells divine. I'm surprised you're thinking of selling this place. It's a great little spot."

I choked on my own spit. *Wow! Not wasting any time, I see.*

The woman's face changed before us, as she took in Finn's comment. The warmth that was there a moment ago vanished, replaced by an expression I couldn't quite discern. If I had to guess, I'd wager she was angry. Raging, even.

I nudged Finn's boot under the table with my own. He didn't flinch.

"How did you know about that?" Edith asked, her voice rising.

"A friend of mine had a run-in with the Whitmore son when he was in town," Finn said. Lying, obviously. "He mentioned it."

Edith grimaced. "You tell your friend to stay far away from the Whitmores," she warned. "Nothing good can come out of making a deal with that family."

"I take it you didn't take the deal?" I asked.

"Of course not, love!" Edith exclaimed. "I would never let my beautiful shop be turned into a soulless condominium complex."

My brows snuck closer together. "Charles Whitmore couldn't have been happy with that."

"I wouldn't know," Edith said. "I only spoke to his snake of a real estate agent. But if the son were to come around, I'd tell him the same thing. I'm not selling. Not now, not ever."

My eyes flicked to Finn's. He gave me a knowing nod as he caught the same thing I did. Edith thought Charles was alive; she had no idea he was dead. Whatever happened to the prodigal son, she had nothing to do with it.

Biting off a chunk of the scone, I moaned as the pieces crumbled in my mouth. The taste was heavenly, and I was glad Edith didn't want to sell her shop. Everyone in town should be privy to these magical scones. When I took a sip of the tea, my eyes widened. It was also quite amazing.

In precaution, I tried to smell out if Edith was a paranormal, but there was no trace of magic in the air. The woman was simply that talented.

As she walked away from our table, I noticed that Finn was yet to try his tea. My nose scrunched as I locked my eyes on him. "Something the matter?"

"I'm more of a coffee person," Finn replied, pushing the tea off to the side.

My stomach twisted up. If I didn't know it before, it was certainly clear now. Finn O'Malley and I would never get along. What person didn't enjoy a good cup of tea?

I watched Finn shift uncomfortably in his chair and took that as a sign to take my time. My face warmed as I slowly brought the cup to my lips and took the slightest of sips. The satisfaction of watching Finn squirm around, eager to leave, was enough to make up for his lack of good taste. I couldn't believe I almost let myself consider anything but the rivalry between us.

Not a tea drinker. Preposterous.

Chapter Fourteen

The wreath smelled of pine and tulips, a new combination for an arrangement I was surprisingly a fan of. The family for today's viewing specifically requested it, and luckily, I had both growing in the garden already. I hung the flowery oval on the stand, nudging it around until it was perfectly centered. Stepping back, I inspected the rest of the room.

Soft lighting bathed the elongated space as the sun streamed in from the three windows alongside one wall. There were tall pedestals with more tulips carefully arranged in them between each window, and I made sure to push those around as well, so they didn't feel oddly spaced out. At the center, past the rows of white chairs, was the casket. Empty for now, until it was time to place dear Mrs. Montair in her final place. The casket was a respectful polished black with an ivory lining. An excellent choice for someone of Mrs. Montair's age. Aside from the occasional bodies delivered by the police, most of my clients died of natural causes and old age.

Mrs. Montair was not an exception.

I smiled, placing the memorial brochures on each of the chairs. It was going to be a lovely service.

"Why are you so happy?"

My smile dropped instantly. I turned to Theo, framed in the doorway, his whiskers and fur limned in the light from the chandelier in the hallway. "Glad to be back to regular business," I said. "Last night I decided that I had enough of running around playing detective with the Wardens."

"You mean you spent too much time with a certain grumpy morgue director, and your crush scared you off?" Theo drawled. "Because what you said sounded different."

"That's because you're wrong," I said defensively. "I am simply not getting involved in a wild goose chase. Besides, Charles died of a heart attack. We have no reason to think anything else about it." I looked down the spotless aisle. "And I have a funeral home to run."

The cat licked the rear of his front paw. "Oh, you're running all right."

I was annoyed by the changeling, and it wasn't even noon yet. Taking a calming breath, I counted to ten, then proceeded to do the final cleaning up of the viewing room before stepping out and closing the door behind me. My head was full of racing thoughts, most of which had nothing to do with Mrs. Montair. Theo was wrong, of course. I had no feelings toward Finn other than frustration, but that wasn't what bothered me so much. What really dug into my nerves was that the cat was right. I was running.

Only not from Finn O'Malley.

No matter how I tried to push it out of my head, Charles's death continued to weigh heavily on me. I couldn't help but think there was more, even though all the evidence pointed to the contrary. It wasn't fairy intuition, nothing of the sort—more of a professional curiosity that I couldn't shake. That and what the tea shop owner said seemed to drag me back to the man in my morgue.

The Whitmores were bad news. Could they have been bad news enough for someone to want Charles dead?

From what I heard so far, it sure seemed like it.

I filled my lungs, teetering backward. My ankle caught on something soft and I stutter-stepped into the wall, my shoulder knocking a picture frame off the nail. It crashed to the ground with a thundering thud.

I gasped as glass shards spread over the hardwood floor.

My eyes narrowed on Theo crouching near to me. "Can you please, for the love of fairy dust, stop sneaking up on me? This will take forever to clean up."

"First of all, I called your name twice, and you didn't hear me," the cat said. "Secondly, why does it matter how long it takes? It's only you and me here—plenty of time to gather this mess up. Not like you have a revolving door of people visiting."

My foot stepped on a pile of glass. I cringed as it shattered into smaller pieces under the weight of my slipper. "It's not a matter of people visiting. I don't care if I ran a hotel—"

The thought tore away from me, words falling in mid-air. I looked at Theo, my face paling. We were having trouble gathering information on Charles and his connection to the town, since most of his dealings have been in King City. I always thought it strange that Charles was here, but no one had seen him or knew who he was. But if he did stay in town, there was one place that would definitely have information on the mysterious real estate mogul.

I clicked my tongue. "Where does one stay when they go on vacation?" I asked Theo.

The changeling glared at me. "Are you drinking with breakfast?"

"Never mind," I told him. "I have to step out for a bit. I'll be back before the service"

"I certainly hope so!" Theo yelled. "Unless you want the guests walking through glass and for the service to be led by a talking cat!"

There was an added chill in the air as the doors of the Rose Hollow Hotel opened to let me in. Thick, ornate carpet lined the mahogany floors, and my feet sank into its plush embrace with every step. To my right was a small seating area with two antique sofas and a wide wood coffee table between them. Several of the hotel's guests sat on the couches, each one busy with either their phone or the pamphlets they grabbed from the side table. Right past the seating area stood a bronze-framed elevator that reminded me of something out of the old movies Theo and I enjoyed watching. There was a gold luggage cart next to it, and an attendant in a red uniform stacked several suitcases atop it. When I passed, he gave me a friendly wave and continued his task.

I wasn't sure what I was expecting to find out, but it was nice to get out of the funeral home for a change of pace. In fact, my eagerness was so intense that I barely noticed the few guests loitering in the lobby. That was until one of the kids playing on the couch started shrieking because her brother took her book. The parents did their best to rectify the situation, and my heart jolted for them as they attempted to maneuver the upset child back to their room, while the other guests gaped at them disapprovingly. Though I didn't have children of my own, I couldn't help but sympathize. Parenting was hard, even on a good day.

I stepped aside to let the family scurry off toward the elevator, then turned to the reception desk where a woman stood typing on a computer. She had a blond bob that was so sleek it made me do a double take, and her posh outfit looked to be out of a magazine or a runway show. She didn't strike me as someone who would normally visit the hotel, let alone work here.

As I approached, I gleaned a brass name plate pinned to her silk blazer. Cilia Craven. I recognized it immediately as the name of the owner of the hotel. Community gossip said that Cilia inherited the hotel from the previous owner after her tragic death. The story was the source of a lot of gossip in town for a while. As it turned out, the last owner was a powerful vampire that was killed while hunting down a wicked witch coven. The details were vague, but she left the hotel to Cilia out of the blue and to the surprise of everyone else. Most assumed the place would have gone to a family member or left in a will. People didn't know why she left it to a member of the staff instead. I assumed it was because there was no other family around. Vampires didn't live forever as the myths stated, but they did kick it around for longer than humans, so if the previous owner was unlucky enough not to find a mate, she'd have been all alone. Unless she found herself a coven of other vampires. But those were rare and few in-between, so I doubted it.

I paused a few feet from the desk, a smell tickling my nostrils. My nose twitched. Cilia Craven was a paranormal.

I didn't know what kind, but she definitely had magic. A sneeze got trapped in my nose. A powerful paranormal at that. Maybe that explained the hotel transaction.

When the hotel owner saw me standing in front of her, she flashed all her teeth. "Welcome to Rose Hollow," she said. "Are you checking in?"

"Um, not really," I replied.

She looked at me as though I had lost the last of my marbles.

Attempting to put her at ease, I relaxed my stance. "I live here in town. Sort of," I said. Her grimace deepened. I really was quite terrible at this, wasn't I? Trying again, I rubbed my forehead and looked at Cilia. "Sorry, let me start over. I'm Lyra Moore and I'm the funeral director at Mistbrook Manor. I'm not sure if you've heard of it."

"Heard of it?" Cilia said, chuckling. "We used to dare each other to knock on the door when we were little. And that was before it became a funeral home!"

Wonderful.

"Is it haunted, like they say?" Cilia asked.

My eyes turned to slits. "Is the hotel?"

"Touché. So, Lyra. If you're not here for a room, how can I help you?"

I checked the lobby to make sure no one was waiting —or listening in—before leaning over the reception desk. My shoulders hiked up and my spine steeled as I said, "There was a body delivered to my morgue a few nights ago. No one seemed to know who it was, but since then, I was able to discover the identity of the man." I cleared my throat, realizing how insane what I was about to ask sounded. "I know it isn't standard practice, but I was hoping you might be able to look him up in your system. It appears he visited our town before and yet no one remembers the man."

"Hmm," Cilia said in a hushed tone.

I bristled. What was I doing? This was a terrible idea, and I never should have come down here. My skin flushed, turning to a bright shade of pink.

"You know what? It's fine. I don't even know why I'm asking. It's a bizarre idea."

Before I could say goodbye and scurry out with my tail between my legs, Cilia reopened the laptop. She typed speedily, her polished nails clicking away quickly. A second later, she asked, "What's his name?"

"Y-you're going to help me?" I stuttered. "Why?"

The hotel owner laughed. "I have a friend that's very similar to you," she explained. "Constantly chasing a mystery. So, what's your guy's name?"

"Charles Whitmore," I said. "Thank you."

A few more clicks and Cilia's forehead began to crease. She stuck her face closer to the screen, tapping away on keys. Lines formed at the corners of her mouth as her lips turned down.

"Interesting," she said. "That doesn't appear to be any record of him. Hang on."

Turning away from me, she ducked under the desk. The sound of things moving rose from beneath, followed by a clunk and a string of curses. Finally, the hotel owner's head popped back up. She rose to stand, a hard drive in her hands.

Plugging it in, she said, "We have all our records online and your guy isn't there. There was a book from nine years ago that looked glitchy, though. It's probably nothing, but I'm going to check the backup in case we missed something."

I waited with my heart in my throat as she booted up the hard drive and clicked on a file on the screen.

Her eyes narrowed, the light emanating from the laptop amplifying her sharp features. Suddenly, Cilia's mouth gaped. "Well, that is odd, isn't it?"

"What is?" I asked.

"On here, room one-forty-four is booked under Charles Whitmore. Nine years ago, almost to the day. Seems he booked it for the full week."

I tried to understand. "Why is that strange?"

Cilia turned the laptop to face me, tapping on the screen. "Because on our most current catalog, the same room was booked for the same date but under a different name. Samuel Thorne."

"That is odd," I agreed. "Has this ever happened before? A glitch in the system?"

"If this is a glitch, then I'm a unicorn," the hotel owner said. "This isn't a computer error. Someone changed the name on the booking."

I swallowed the saliva that pooled in my hot mouth. "Who would do that, and why?"

"I have no clue. It was before my time at the hotel," the owner said. "But if you want to follow up, Samuel's shop is right up the street. Over by the old boatyard."

"Samuel lives in town?"

She nodded. "Sure does. He's actually my mechanic. Great service at a price you can't beat," she said. "That's literally his motto."

As she continued to chat about the mechanic and

why he's such a wonderful addition to the town, my mind wandered. There was a small chance that the booking was, in fact, glitching, and yet I couldn't fathom that being the case. Charles Whitmore had been in town before, and someone out there wanted that information erased. Not only that, but they had the means to change the booking. Either they worked at the hotel or had access to someone who did. The mystery surrounding Charles continued to grow, the deeper I dug. And it now appeared I had more questions than answers, the opposite of what I wished out of this day trip.

After confirming with Cilia that no one else from that time still worked at the hotel, I thanked her for all the help and stepped outside. My vision spotted briefly, refocusing on my truck parked across the street.

Perhaps it was time to get my car checked by a professional. Surely it was due for an inspection.

Chapter Fifteen

The universe must have known what I was up to. A few blocks from the boatyard, my old truck started to growl—a deep, cranky rumble that made it sound as though it was channeling Theo's disapproval when I forgot to buy him salami. The truck sputtered, the engine wheezing and rattling like a Victorian patient struggling through a serious case of whooping cough. I clenched the steering wheel, willing it to last a couple more minutes, but the dashboard lights flickered ominously, as if warning me I was already past my welcome.

With a final shudder and an alarming pop, the engine quit entirely, leaving me stranded right in front of Samuel Thorne's shop. I exhaled, reaching for my keys to pull them out, but froze when I noticed a thin, ominous ribbon of smoke rising from beneath the hood. *Great.* It appeared that my truck was going up in dramatic fashion—as though it had been rehearsing for this moment in some smoky theatrical production.

I took a few tentative steps back, half expecting an explosion or a shower of bolts to follow. My heart pounded in my chest as I watched the smoke rise, wondering if my truck was about to become a makeshift bomb that I'd be tasked with disarming.

"Made it right in time," a hoarse voice said from up the driveway.

I shielded my eyes from the sun and looked past the smoke to the man standing in front of an open garage door. His tight curls were cut close to his head and he had a thick beard that had several grays in it. The man wore oil-stained coveralls, and a torn white tee underneath them. He seemed entirely oblivious to the cold, his brow covered in sweat. In his hand, he held a large wrench, and I noticed a shiny new car raised on a hydraulic lift in the garage behind him.

There was no mistaking that this was Samuel Thorne. The mechanic.

I left my truck to its agonizing death and approached Samuel. Rubbing the rear of my neck, I smiled sheepishly. "Lucky timing," I said. "You're Samuel, right? The owner of the shop?"

"One and the same," the mechanic said jovially.

"I can't tell you how glad I am that you're open. I don't know what I'd do without a car."

"Don't know if you'll be doing much driving in it now," Samuel said. "Likely for the best with the storm coming."

My head tilted to gaze at the blue sky above. All this talk about the storm, but the weather didn't seem to change much to me. Although I had been too occupied to notice if we did get snowed in. The situation revolving around Charles's death had a vise grip on me the likes of which I hadn't experienced before. I wondered if this was how the Wardens felt all the time, this innate need to dig further.

I brushed off the thought and looked at Samuel. "Right, of course," I agreed. "Any chance you might be able to take a look at it now?"

Samuel wiped his brow with the back of his overalls. A black smear covered his skin from the oil on the fabric, and I fought the urge to wipe it off. *Don't go touching strangers now.* I did not need a restraining order, especially not from the man who was my only means of getting the truck back up and running.

"I don't know," he said. "It looks to be a big job."

My face collapsed in disappointment.

"On second thought," Samuel said, seeing how distraught I was. "Let me see what we're working with. Could be I'm wrong."

As he ambled over to the truck, I did a little happy hop behind his back. If I was any more relieved, my wings might have popped out to celebrate. Paranoia tickled my skin. I patted my shoulder blades, slumping when I didn't feel the wings there.

Plumes of dark smoke covered Samuel as he popped open the hood. He waved a dirty rag to clear it, but it only made the smoke spread more, rising like storm clouds all around him.

With practice ease, Samuel put one foot on the grill guard and hoisted himself to peer inside. The smell of oil and charred metal made my stomach turn.

Samuel reached into the beast and rattled on a part I couldn't make out from where I stood. His face darkened.

"Is it serious?"

The mechanic hopped off the grill guard and stalked toward me. He tossed the rag over his shoulder, his eyes narrowing. "Looks to be a fault somewhere in your fuel injection system."

"I have no idea what that means," I admitted.

Samuel chuckled. "It's nothing that can't be fixed. But I won't know if there's another issue unless I check it out thoroughly, which could take some time."

My spine curved as I slumped. "How much do you reckon?"

"A couple days for sure," Samuel replied.

No matter how much I wished for another outcome, I really couldn't blame the man for any of this. He was doing his best to help me out, and I hadn't even revealed the real reason I was here.

Which was beginning to sound incredibly unhinged, if I was honest.

I nodded. "Do you need a deposit of some sort? I can leave the truck here and give you my number for when it's ready."

As I handed him my card, I saw the surprise on his face brighten his features. He tapped on the cardboard, slicking it in oil until it resembled his clothes and forehead. "You work at the funeral home up on those cliffs?" he asked.

"Own it, actually," I said.

"Well, what do you know? Far drive from my place. How did you end up all the way down by the water?"

A harsh wind looped around my hair and tossed it into my face. I spit out the strands, clearing my mouth from them so I could answer. "You were recommended by Cilia Craven. From the Rose Hollow Hotel."

Was it me, or was that panic that flashed across the mechanic's features? It appeared I hit a nerve. Now it was time to push some buttons.

"I have some family coming to town and was thinking of putting them in a room so they wouldn't have to stay in the funeral home," I said, lying. "The owner said you spent some time at the hotel. What did you think of it?"

Before me, Samuel's fingers twitched, clenching and unclenching, as if unable to find a place to rest. His breath came in shallow bursts, each one quicker than the last, until he was nearly gasping. What was happening here? The man was clearly having a panic attack. His eyes flicked around the driveway, looking anywhere but me.

The sweat he wiped from his brow returned, and his nervous energy was palpable.

I couldn't let this go on. I had to put the poor guy out of his misery. He was clearly involved in the cover-up of the booking or he wouldn't be acting so remarkably guilty right now. But why?

I pressed my hands to my temples, saying, "I know you didn't stay at the Rose Hollow."

"What? No. Of course I did," Samuel argued. His chest deflated with an expelled breath. "How did you know?"

"It doesn't matter. What matters is that the person who did stay in that room is dead and something about this entire thing doesn't seem right to me," I told the mechanic. "If you know anything at all, please tell me. Why did your name end up on the paperwork for the room originally booked by Charles Whitmore nine years ago?"

Samuel sighed, his entire body crumpling. He looked at me with the face of someone much older than his thirty-some years, with lines around his eyes so deep they probably hurt.

His lips puckered, and he gestured to the garage behind him. "I was going to lose the shop," he said finally. "Nine years ago, I was going to lose my entire livelihood. When that young man brought his car here that night in September, I was on my final days. The bank was knocking down my door and the bills were stacking up. So, when he offered me all that money to fix the car, no questions asked, I did it."

The surrounding air turned heavy and thick. A breeze stirred, faint at first, but it gained speed quickly and my hair was a tornado once more. Overhead, the sun that was out before ducked behind a gloomy dark cloud that rolled in like a churning wave.

My skin rippled from the onset of frigidness that settled over the driveway.

Gaze sharpening, I pointed my nose at the mechanic. "What does any of that have to do with the hotel booking?"

"The young man whose car I fixed was Charles Whitmore," he replied. "And a few days later, I got a call from someone claiming to be some big shot lawyer from the city that worked for the Whitmore estate. He said the Whitmores were going to triple the sum Charles paid me if I let them put my name down. Pretend that I was the one who took out the room."

I arched my brow. "And you agreed?"

"I did. I had no choice, though if I had to do it over again, I'd have never taken the deal."

"Why not?" I asked, my interest peaking.

The mechanic's shoulders shook. He bit his lower lip, chewing on it hard enough to draw blood. His amber eyes burnt into me, and I suddenly felt the need to run away.

"The car I fixed, the shiny new Mercedez," Samuel said. "Charles told me he hit a deer going too fast near the hiking trails. Said that he couldn't afford the headache of dealing with a speeding ticket, so he wanted me to make the car look brand new."

I sucked in a sharp breath. "That's odd, but not an unreasonable request."

"That's not it," Samuel said in desperation. "I've been fixing cars for almost my whole life. This shop was my dad's, and his before him. It's why I couldn't risk losing it. You can imagine I've seen my fair share of deer hits." He rubbed his bloodshot eyes with the rag. "Whatever that young man hit that night, it was no deer. No, ma'am. It was no animal at all, I reckon."

Chapter Sixteen

It was almost impossible to have a proper conversation with a dead person. I stared at Charles Whitmore's lifeless body on the slab and frowned.

"What did you do last time you visited our town, Charles?"

Similar to the several times I asked before, Charles had no reply. It didn't stop me from continuing to badger him. I always found that talking things out with myself helped me process and this time, I could talk to someone else instead. Well, sort of. Sure, Charles was cold as ice, but Theo was nowhere to be found, and I had to make sense of what I found out.

After the taxi dropped me off from the mechanic

shop, all I could think about was the accident Samuel revealed.

My hand dropped from the metal slab. "What happened that night?" I asked the dead man before me. "Something bad that your family had to cover up. What did you hit if it wasn't a deer?"

I swallowed.

"Or who?"

Stepping away, I paced the length of the morgue and returned to Charles. With his eyes closed and his body positioned to resemble a deep sleep, he looked so peaceful. So serene. Not at all like the person I was slowly starting to realize he was. It was true what they said then: money could buy your way out of trouble, even the kind that should have you behind bars.

I grimaced.

I was jumping to conclusions. All I had was the word of a local mechanic and a booking that had been tampered with. Sure, it didn't look good on paper, but it wasn't enough. If I wanted to bring evidence to the police that could help us get to the bottom of what happened to Charles Whitmore—and I did—I had to find more. Besides, it was beginning to look that there may have been another case that might need the attention of the cops. One that likely no one knew about.

Another thing bothered me about the new discovery

that formed even more questions. If it was true that Charles had a serious accident that required an illegal cover up, why return here? The Whistling Kettle was a cute spot and in a prime location, but was buying it worth risking someone recognizing Charles? He could have easily let the real estate agent handle the purchase. As Arthur said, they did most of their deals over the phone anyhow.

Then why show up?

I checked the cellphone that lay on the desk in the corner. I should really tell the police about this. Let them figure it out.

As I debated my next move, the screen flashed with an incoming message. I gave Charles one quick glance, then pushed away from the slab to pick up the phone. My eyes rounded as I read the message.

"Finn?"

How did the morgue director get my number and why was he texting me? We weren't exactly on friendly terms. Reading what he said, my stomach dropped into my shoes. My back grew rigid.

I looked at the body in the room. "Your tox report came back," I told Charles.

Fingers gliding over the keys, I typed a message back to Finn. *What does it say?*

Three blue dots flashed on the screen, followed by a text bubble.

Let's talk in person. Can you meet at the mausoleum?

My jaw locked, but I nodded as I wrote, *Be there in fifteen minutes. See you soon.*

Tucking Charles back into the mortuary cabinet, I ran upstairs. My feet padded on the floor as I rushed toward the front door, grabbing for my car keys on instinct. It took me a second to clear my head and remember that I was stranded for the foreseeable future, then another twenty minutes until a taxi arrived in the driveway. Checking for Theo one last time, I got into the backseat and watched the manor disappear from view as the driver took me to the cemetery.

Thanking her, I jumped out eagerly and bolted down the winding path between the graves. My heart raced as I neared the mausoleum. I wondered what could have been so important that Finn wouldn't talk on the phone. Something must have triggered him enough to message me in the first place.

Unless the others were there too.

I relaxed a little, realizing that was probably the case. It didn't make sense for Finn to ask for my help when he had the Wardens on his side. They were a team. I was a random fairy that infiltrated their secret society like a complete sociopath.

When I approached the Starling family mausoleum, I paused. The shadow of a figure hovered not far from the building. My lungs stopped working. All I could see from here were wide shoulders and long legs.

Fear tripped down my spine.

The figure was standing only two feet from the portal. The same portal I hadn't reinforced in days since I was too busy chasing leads.

It can't be.

Tears burned my eyes and spotted my vision. Legs shaking, I took a slow step toward the figure, my nerve skyrocketing. As I walked, an ache formed between my temples and my ears rang in alarm.

Did he finally find me? Was this the end?

I gathered whatever courage I had left and walked up to the man. Relief flowed through me instantly.

My brow creased, and I stepped closer. "Finn?"

The morgue director spun around, his eyes blazing. He resembled a panicked animal and for a second, I thought I imagined him asking to meet him here. Fidgeting his fingers, he shoved his hands in the pocket of his leather jacket and looked at the ground next to him. No, not at the ground. At a gravestone.

I followed his gaze.

"Is that...?"

"Jenny," he replied solemnly.

My heart sank. In all my traipsing around the cemetery, it never occurred to me that Finn's wife would be buried here in Orchard Hollow. I knew her family was from town, thus the mausoleum, but for some reason I assumed her grave would be closer to her home with Finn a few towns over. I stood stock still. This was why he kept returning here. It wasn't the Wardens, or not entirely. Being in the cemetery gave Finn a chance to visit his dead wife.

And here I was thinking he was odd for wanting to meet here today.

I pressed my lips together and placed a hand on his arm. "It will get easier one day," I whispered. "That void, it will never go away, but it will get easier. I promise."

"It already has," Finn replied. "When Jenny first got diagnosed, I was so angry. With the cancer, with the lack of help out there, even with her for not being angry alongside me. But Jenny, she was something else. She stayed strong until the very end...kept me grounded."

I smiled. "Wow. I wish I'd gotten to meet her. She sounds really wonderful."

"She truly was. That's why I stuck it out with the Wardens all this time. Because it was what she wanted." His brow creased. "Look, I know I probably came off harshly. But I'm not good with change."

"I get it," I said. "I was a stranger infiltrating the ranks. Not sure if you noticed, but I'm not all that great with people. I'm sure I didn't give you much reason to trust me."

The wind trilled around us and the trees rustled like whispers in the distance. Above our heads, a flock of birds took off, their wings flapping. A strong wind carried them farther away. I tugged on my scarf, hiding my exposed skin from the harsh elements enveloping the cemetery.

My eyes met Finn's. I suddenly realized my hand was still on his arm, and squeezing. I unfurled my fingers, skin flushed and red.

Finn cleared his throat. "Um, well. Thank you for coming out so quickly. I wasn't sure you'd be up for it."

"Not a problem," I replied, my voice breathy and hoarse. "Are the others downstairs?"

Finn nodded. "I called everyone over as soon as I got the report back. It's...strange."

"How so?"

He reached into his jacket breast pocket to pull out a folded piece of paper. As he handed it to me, I avoided touching his fingers for fear of what it might rouse again. There was no time to waste on crushes. Especially not on someone like the morgue director, who clearly was not yet over his wife.

Clutching the paper, I unfolded it and read the report. My throat was suddenly bone dry. I looked at Finn through my lashes. "This can't be right," I said. "It says here there were high traces of digitoxin, the same amount we would see in patients who take it regularly."

"As I said, strange."

I didn't understand.

"The only way that Charles would have digitoxin in his system was if he was using it to treat a heart condition."

Before me, Finn gave one curt nod in agreement. "I contacted his doctor in the city. He was being treated for heart arrhythmia. Has been on the stuff since college."

The ground gave out under me. Everything we learned so far was starting to come together. Finn and I were right to think something fishy was going on. What happened to Charles wasn't natural. And it certainly was no accident.

I swallowed, patting my chest to clear the blockage under my ribcage. Sucking in a jagged breath, I clutched Finn's arm again.

"If Charles Whitmore was on digitoxin," I said softly. "How the heck did he have a heart attack?"

Chapter Seventeen

A book slammed shut in the darkened space between two tall bookcases. It was followed by a string of curses, which was followed by another string of curses when the first one proved to be insufficient. A moment later, Ellie emerged. Her hair was a short curly mess that jutted out in every direction, and her glasses sat so low on her nose that I worried they might fall away any second. She ran her long fingers through the curls, tugged at them when they got trapped in the hive of hair.

Ellie let out an exasperated moan.

"No luck in the newspaper archives?" Rosemary asked, barely looking up from her laptop.

While Ellie was looking for possible accidents

around the time Charles visited Orchard Hollow last, the rest of the Wardens, me included, sat around the large table in the center of their hideaway. Each one busied themselves on a different part of the research that could lead us to the next clue. Since the discovery of Charles's heart condition and the treatment he was receiving for it, everyone in the group agreed that there was more at play in his death than we originally thought.

More than anyone knew about, at least.

With that in mind, we had spent the past few hours scouring every source we could think of. Finn focused on police reports, tapping into his connections with the local police. A surprise to me, considering he worked in a morgue in a completely different town. Apparently, his brother-in-law was a cop on the force here. Convenient.

While he worked on the reports, Rosemary and Mortimer opted for the online stalking route. They checked every blog post, every website, and every link they could grasp that crossed Charles's path nine years ago.

I, on the other hand, focused on the science. My main goal was to try to make sense of Charles's apparent heart attack, and to see if it was remotely plausible he could have one while on controlled doses of digitoxin. According to what I read so far, it was possible but highly unlikely, since the medication would work to prevent heart failure. Digitoxin doses were created to be longer lasting, meant to not only treat heart conditions like the one Charles had, but to make his heart stronger. It was quite literally used to treat heart failure. Either the medication didn't do its job or something else was at play here.

Ellie rolled her eyes, walked over, and poured herself into an empty chair at the table. She looked at Rosemary, then at each of us. "Would it have killed the Orchard Hollow Gazette to embrace the modern age and upload their issues online?" She ground her teeth. "I've checked and double-checked the printed archives, and there is nothing noted during the time of his visit. I even went as far back as the year prior and six months after his visit. Not a peep."

"I can't believe you all have the entirety of the Gazette's archives here," I said. "Don't those belong in the library?"

Ellie pushed her glasses up with her index finger. "They're copies. I used to date one of the librarians, and she wasn't great at locking things up."

"She sure had you in a lock," Rosemary muttered.

Ellie chuckled. "You saw those cheekbones, Rosie," she said. "You know I'm a sucker for good bone structure."

"A mortician obsessed with bones?" Mortimer asked. "How odd."

The three burst into a fit of laughter. My lips curled up and before I knew it, I was giggling along with them. There was a lightness in the air despite what we were doing in the mausoleum, and it made the clenching vise on my chest loosen. It was strange. We were ten feet underground and yet I'd never breathed easier.

My eyes crinkled and met Finn's smiling gaze. A flush heated my skin. I tamped it down, but the warmth of his attention remained and lingered even as my lungs refused to work. *Not this again.*

I cleared my throat, that was suddenly hot and dry. "Anything in the police reports?" I asked him.

"Not a thing. If Charles hit something other than a deer, it wasn't reported."

"Could there be a chance you're missing a file?"

Finn crooked a bushy brow at me. "I know you don't know him, but trust me when I tell you, Jenny's brother is not one to miss anything," he said. "At our wedding he spent a half-hour straightening every flower arrangement that, and I quote, *felt too imperfect for the day.* He has a thing for details."

"Got it." I looked at Mortimer and Rosemary. "How about you two?"

Rosemary shrugged as she clicked away on her laptop. Sitting next to her and scrolling on the world's largest tablet, Mortimer said, "Well, the Whitmores are not great people. Very rich people, but not the most humanitarian of the bunch."

"How so?" Finn asked.

"There's a lot of documented cases of them doing whatever it took to get a deal done. Once portraying them really walking the line of what's legally acceptable. There's enough here to write an entire biography on the family's awful business practices."

Across from me, Ellie guffawed. "I bet that book would be a bestseller. People love drama."

I couldn't help but think she was right. Our little group was a prime example of how much humans needed to know about other people. Humans and fairies alike, it seemed.

"The last high-rise Charles built was dubbed 'Hell Condos' online. Several people tried to sue the family for not having proper safety features in place and cutting corners to save costs, yet nothing came out of it."

I shivered. "It was that bad?"

"A woman's windows fell out" Rosemary answered.

"Wow. That's...bad, all right."

There was a hushed agreement amongst the group. We stayed quiet for a while, processing the information. While I desperately wanted to find out what happened to Charles Whitmore, I was starting to doubt if I should. The more I learned of him and his family, the less I wanted to know. Not that it would stop me from getting to the bottom of things. All life was precious, and all deserved justice.

Unlike most other fae, I valued honesty. Even if it did belong to a man who may not have deserved it.

"What did you get on the meds?" Ellie asked, jarring me from my thoughts.

I turned in my chair to face her. The light of the overhead chandelier cast gloomy shadows under her glasses, making her appear like she was getting ready to tell ghost stories. The way her eyes clocked every tiny move I made had my nerves rattling under my skin. The woman did not trust me. Which was bizarre. Finn himself was starting to warm up to me, and he was my biggest critic. What did I do to make her so wary of me?

More importantly, why did I care?

A single thought ran through my head, making my stomach twist into knots. I liked it here. In the gloomy mausoleum under the cemetery, with this odd combination of people. For the first time since I left Fairy, I felt like I belonged.

Ellie gave the table a loud knock. "Hello? The meds?"

"Sorry. Spaced out," I said. "Nothing we didn't already know. The chances of Charles having a heart attack while on digitoxin are quite low. Perhaps impossible."

The mortician clucked her tongue. "Is there

anything that could mimic a heart attack? Enough so that it wouldn't cause suspicion in an autopsy?"

"I thought of that too," I admitted. "But no. If Charles was given any drugs to trigger a heart attack, they would have shown up in the tox report."

"Well, we'll keep at it. Something is bound to present itself," Mortimer said encouragingly. "Do not fret, team!"

We spent another hour on our respective research topics before calling it a day. I had to get back home to feed Theo, and the rest of the group had their respective lives to run. As I climbed the stairs and stepped into the cold air of the cemetery, I couldn't help but smile. We may not have been any closer to finding out what happened to Charles, yet today did not feel like a complete waste.

I spent hours in the company of people, and I didn't once wish to be elsewhere. This was new for me. I couldn't wait to get home to tell Theo about it.

Skipping over piles of snow, I trekked back to the parking lot. The hair on the rear of my neck rose as the feeling that I wasn't alone crept in. My eyes scanned the cemetery at my back, coming up empty. Nose to the sky, I gave the air a quick sniff, but all I sensed was the pines around me and a faint hint of lilacs, probably from one of the arrangements on a grave.

No magic nearby.

Giving the area another scan, I tightened the belt on my coat and hurried to the taxi waiting for me in the lot. As I got into the backseat and closed the door, the worry dissipated, vanishing alongside the cemetery in the window as we drove away. *Almost home,* I told myself. *Finally.*

Chapter Eighteen

The first thing I noticed when I woke up this morning was the wonderful display of torn socks Theo left me in the front hallway. The next was the voicemail on my phone and three missed calls that preceded it. I listened to the message, my mood going from sour to relieved in seconds.

"What's happening to your face?" Theo asked.

I kicked one of the socks at him, but missed the mark entirely. The woolen tube hung from the lampshade it landed on, illuminated by the glow from within as if to taunt me further. My lips dropped from the grin holding them hostage. "It's called happiness," I told the cat. "You should try it sometimes. And stop stealing my socks. It's weird."

"They make for good bird nests," Theo said.

My eyes narrowed. "What?" The sudden realization that every sock was missing its pair made my skin crawl. "Theo, where are the others?"

"Never mind that. Why are you so happy this morning?"

I started to press him further, but the cat had already moved on and was walking figure eights between my legs. I rolled my eyes skyward and allowed him to push me into the kitchen and away from the sock pile. A later discussion to be had.

When we were in the kitchen, I put on the kettle and prepped a mug with the strongest tea I could find. Then I sat down with Theo at the table, waiting until the changeling got settled in a chair before saying, "I got a call from the mechanic. The truck is ready for pickup!"

"That's what you're so excited about?" Theo asked. "It's a car, Lyra."

"It's my way to get around," I corrected. "And in case you haven't seen outside yet, the weather is getting bad out there. You'll be glad to have that truck if we have to evacuate for the storm."

Theo wiggled his whiskers, stuck his tail out, and jumped down, his interest fading quickly. He shot a quick glance my way as he made his way out of the kitchen. "Pick up more whipped cream while you're out," the cat said, disappearing around the corner.

With him gone, the silence of the manor felt so dense it pressed in on me, an invisible weight settling over my skin, sinking down to my bones. It wasn't a comforting silence, the sort I used to savor when free from the changeling's constant presence. In the morgue, silence was an ally, a stillness that made work feel precise and meditative. But here, alone in the kitchen, it seemed different—thick and oppressive, the kind that left a chill lingering in the air.

The last few days with the Wardens had filled every corner of my mind with sound and purpose, but now the emptiness had returned tenfold. My skin prickled as I looked down the endless corridor stretching before me. Had the manor always been so eerie? Surely I'd known every inch of it, every shadow cast by the flickering lamps on the walls, and yet now, it felt as though unseen dangers lurked just out of sight, watching.

The heavy velvet curtains blocked out all but slivers of sun. Shadows twisted into something almost alive, shifting as the light played tricks on my vision. I swallowed hard, straining to hear any sound that wasn't my own breathing.

Nothing came. Not even Theo.

I downed the tea despite it being hot, and ran upstairs to get ready. If I hurried, I could get a taxi up here fast enough to pick up the truck and have time to stop by the Whistling Kettle for an afternoon cup of that

Double Cream Earl Gray. Now that I thought about getting out, I was surprisingly eager to spend the day outdoors before the weather turned for the worst. Maybe after the stop in town I could put in an hour in the garden.

The plans for the day played out in my head as I wrangled my messy hair into a high bun and crammed myself into several layers of sweaters. Skipping the last step, I landed on the bottom floor again in time to see the headlights of the taxi pull up front.

"You want to come with me?" I yelled out to Theo.

"Not even if you paid me!" the cat replied from the living room.

A second later, the sound of the television being turned on pushed against my back as I left the manor and locked up.

I chuckled. "Enjoy the movie marathon, Theo," I whispered under my breath, and climbed into the car.

My eyes followed the dots of red lining the driveway as we drove away from the manor. The roses had bloomed fuller in the last few days despite me not aiding them with my magic. It seemed remarkable for flowers to thrive so wonderfully this time of year. Visitors were amazed by how I was able to keep the blooms rich and vibrant all year round. I would never tell them, of course. As far as the town was concerned, I was a miracle gardener.

I narrowed my eyes at a bush on the far end of the property alongside the cliff drop-off. I could have sworn that one only had buds yesterday. Shaking my head, I averted my attention. I must have been mistaken. Either that or I was better with green magic these days.

Whatever the reason, it was a welcome surprise.

The water lapped the shore beyond the cliffs, and I could hear it even with the windows rolled up. The sea sounded angrier today. Wilder and more unapologetic, awaiting the storm.

The lolling of the taxi as the road vined along made my muscles relax and the knots in my spine vanish. I must have dozed off because the next thing I knew, the car had stopped, and my forehead knocked against the window with a thud.

I rubbed at the throbbing red mark on my skin, paid the driver, and slinked out of the back seat. Glancing around, I spotted my truck near the closed garage door, but Samuel Thorne was nowhere in sight.

I checked the car door. Locked.

"Samuel?" I called out.

When there was no answer, I peered into the single narrow opening in the garage door, seeing only darkness and the glint of tools on a workbench from the light streaming in.

Strange. I was certain the mechanic's message said he would be here when I picked the truck up. Besides, I definitely needed the keys if I was going to drive it home.

I skirted around the side of the garage and toward the small, narrow house a few feet away. The building had faded red paint and white trim around the windows and door that all showed the same signs of age. A rusty sign above the door read "Welcome Home," a chain holding it in place. Barely. Above the sign was a steeply pitched roof, and an old metal chimney that poked out of one side. To the right of the house sat a covered carport with a few scattered tools around it. Though there was no car there now, I had the feeling Samuel often brought his work home with him. Easy to do when the two structures were erected so close together.

As I rounded the main building, a face popped out from behind the slatted wall, making me jump back in terror. I clutched my chest, a scream escaping my lips.

Catching my breath, I placed one hand on the wall and looked at Samuel. "Geez! You scared the life out of me."

"Sorry, Miss Moore," Samuel said, his eyebrows drawn in apologetically. "I was just about to come up front to meet you."

I looked at the quaint home I stood beside. "Cute place you have here."

Samuel's face scrunched. "Thank you. My grandfather built this house by hand. I do my best to keep it standing." He wiped his forehead and nodded to the garage. "Come on, I'll walk back with you."

When we reached my truck, Samuel pulled the keys and handed them over. His lips were pulled tight, and he continued to fidget with the rag tied to his belt loop as I climbed into the car and started it up. The engine purred to life, an epic improvement from before.

"You are a miracle worker," I told the mechanic.

"Happy to help," Samuel said. He patted the side of the car, taking a step back so I could pull out. "I fixed your glove compartment handle too. On the house."

I grimaced. I hadn't realized it was broken.

Paying the deposit and thanking him, I pulled away from the garage and started the journey into town. I could already taste the delicious tea from the Whistling Kettle, and the central street wasn't on the horizon yet. As I drove, I kept thinking about what Samuel said about the glove box. How did he figure out the handle was broken, anyway?

Something was off about that entire interaction. It was almost as though Samuel was trying to tell me a secret without actually saying it.

I checked the rearview to make sure there were no other cars on the road and pulled onto the shoulder. My attention zeroed in on the glove box. There was no way the handle broke without me knowing. I usually tossed my business receipts in there and took them out every week to do the paperwork for the morgue. And I had only recently finished a supply run.

If the handle was broken, I'd certainly would have seen it then.

I reached for the handle and gave it a good twist. The compartment opened up smoothly before me. My eyes rounded.

"What is that?"

Eagerly, I reached for the tattered piece of paper lying on top of my receipt pile. As I unfolded it and laid it flat on the passenger seat, my pulse raced. I smacked my dry lips together. Eyes scanning the words, I tried to swallow, but my mouth was rougher than sandpaper.

Shivers tripped down my body. I had to call the Wardens. Now.

Chapter Nineteen

The crumpled paper lay flat on the coffee table in the manor's living room. I watched it with a side-eye like it was a criminal I'd caught in a citizen's arrest. Sitting rigidly on the loveseat, Theo's gaze drifted from me to the paper, his ears pointed.

I sighed.

"When are they coming?" the cat asked.

His words dragged me from the confines of my over-worked brain and back into the room. I checked the grandfather clock ticking away in the corner. "Finn said he could get everyone here in a few hours. They should arrive shortly."

"Remind me again why the creepy circus is coming here instead of you meeting them in the crypt?"

"Mausoleum," I corrected. "Crypt makes it sound morbid. And they're not creepy."

The cat shrugged, his paws stretching out in front of him. The motion made the tuft of fur on his chest puff out until he looked like he was wearing an Elizabethan neck collar. Theo looked at me with uninterested eyes. "It's all a matter of semantics with you, isn't it?"

"All I'm saying is they are actually very lovely people, and last I checked, cats in glass houses shouldn't throw stones."

The clock chimed to signal two in the afternoon.

"I should message Finn again," I said.

Near me, Theo yawned. "What is so urgent about an old obituary that you have to drag the crypt keepers into our home in the middle of the day?"

I groaned. "I wasn't sure how long they'd be, since they all have jobs," I explained. "It made the most sense to come home. But how do you not see the importance of this?" I waved the piece of paper in the air. "The mechanic left this—I know it."

"And that's super exciting because..."

I slammed the paper down on the table, pointing at the date. "This man died on November twentieth, nine years ago today," I said. "In a hit-and-run, two towns over. Fine Bay. The police there never found the culprit."

The doorbell rang right as Theo's eyebrows arched

in understanding. I nodded, walking away toward the front of the manor. Outside the door, I could hear the familiar voices of the Wardens as I approached, and my steps lightened and quickened to get to them. I plastered on a smile and opened the door.

The group huddled on the front porch, watching me in amazement. All but Finn darted their eyes around the property. I assumed he had his fair share of inspecting the place when he broke in last time.

My posture straightened. "Hi everyone. Welcome to Mistbrook Manor."

"Quite the place you have here," Mortimer said.

I snickered. "It makes for good conversation."

"I bet," Ellie said. She nudged her chin at the cliffs. "Has anyone ever gone over the side?"

"Ellie! Stop it!" Rosemary yelped, elbowing her friend in the ribs.

I waved her off. Wiggling my eyebrows, I locked eyes with Ellie and said, "There's always a first for everything. Care to take a closer look?"

The group erupted in laughter. Ellie's ears burned bright red, and she swiped at her eyes with the soft part of her palms. Her chest rose up and down with hard yips. "All right, new girl. You can stay."

I was about to tell her I had no intention of doing so, but held back. Instead, I opened the door wide and held my arm out, beckoning the Wardens into my home. My heart swelled with every *ooh* and *ah* they uttered as they trotted through the manor. Mortimer stopped to inspect every detail of the woodwork, while Ellie and Rosemary asked about possible murders each time they entered a room. Their disappointment when I told them no one had ever died in the house was palpable.

It wasn't until we reached the living room that I realized Finn had not yet said a word. I pulled on his sleeve, holding him back from the others as they piled into the room.

"Why are you so quiet?" I asked.

He rubbed the rear of his muscular neck, his jaw setting. "Are you safe living here alone in the middle of nowhere?"

"I'm not alone." I pointed to Theo on the loveseat. The cat was begrudgingly making space for Mortimer to sit down, and I could sense his frustration with each scratch of a claw across the velvet. "And yes, I'm perfectly safe. I can take care of myself. Why do you ask?"

Finn bristled. "The thing is, I was wrong about you. I know you said you were only helping us because of Charles Whitmore, but I think—" he paused, "—I think you should consider extending that timeline."

"Finn, are you asking me to join your secret society?"

He winked. I hated that the ice around my heart melted ever so slightly from it.

"I talked to the others, and it was unanimous," he said. "If you feel like becoming a member of...whatever we are, we'd love to have you."

I quirked a brow. "Unanimous? Even Ellie?"

He nodded.

The sound of murmured conversation drifted toward us from the living room. I looked at each one of them, considering Finn's invitation. It was so easy to decline. I could simply walk away and continue my life as I had been—on my own and safe. Then why couldn't I bring myself to do it?

I hated to admit that the four oddballs burrowed through all my defenses. For the first time since I came to this realm, I wished for a life that wasn't quite so solitary. One where it wasn't me, Theo, the roses, and a few dead bodies, day in and day out. A life that mattered.

Of course, I wanted to join the Wardens. It should have been a dead giveaway when I discovered that Charles—

My thoughts fell away, eyes locking onto the piece of paper on the coffee table. I pushed past Finn and into the living room with hurried steps. "Charles Whitmore killed a man in a hit-and-run and his family covered it up," I blurted out.

"Come again?" Ellie asked.

I cleared my parched throat and faced the group, my shoulders taut and my spine straight as an arrow. "A mechanic left that for me to find," I said calmly. "It doesn't matter how, but it was the same man that was hired to fix the car Charles tore apart when he ran over a man nine years ago." I looked at Finn. "It was also the same man whose name was on a reservation at the Rose Hollow Hotel. A reservation that belonged to Charles. The mechanic was offered a lot of money to pretend he stayed there that night, so it would appear that Charles was never in town."

"But he was? In town?" Rosemary asked.

I swallowed, nodding. "He most definitely was." I picked up the obituary from the table and showed it to the group. "And I'm certain he killed this man. Greg Stollen."

There was a long pause while everyone took in what I said. Mortimer and Finn exchanged knowing looks, while Ellie and Rosemary took the obituary and read it thoroughly, holding the paper between them as their eyes danced over the words. After a long enough time to give me the jitters, Mortimer untied his bowtie with a sigh. He rubbed his temples, staring at me through hooded eyes.

"If this is true, there is a very good chance that Charles's death wasn't an accident."

"But he had a heart attack," Rosemary said.

Mortimer sighed again...this time, the expelled breath hung in the air before him in a cloud. I checked to see if any windows had been left open, but the drop in temperature was probably only the manor acting up again. Old houses were tricky to keep up with.

The mortician took the obituary from the women. "We need to find out how someone could induce a heart attack, and we need to do so immediately. I am convinced the death of this poor man and Charles are connected. A domino effect, if you will."

"You're saying someone killed him in revenge," I said.

Mortimer pressed his lips together. "An eye for an eye," he agreed.

He and I were on the same page. Or on the same obituary, as it would seem. I was about to ask Mortimer how we would go about finding the murder weapon when we hadn't had any success doing so thus far, but was interrupted by the doorbell ringing. My ears perked. Who was that?

It was midday, so truthfully it could have been anybody. I forced my body to relax and pushed all negative thoughts out of my head. Excusing myself, I walked to the front door, my belly dropping with every single step. When I twisted the knob, I nearly gagged in my mouth.

Before me, a man with a wide-brimmed hat stood

with his arms crossed and a fermented expression on his tanned face. His thick mustache curled at the edges and his eyes were cast in shadow with only a glint in each as he approached me. I didn't have to ask who it was. Everyone in town knew the sheriff.

"Sheriff Romero," I said curtly. "What brings you by?"

"Good afternoon, Lyra. Sorry to interrupt your day," the sheriff replied. "I was in the area and thought I'd stop by to deliver the news."

Sweat licked at my skin. The clashing wind made it feel like icicles clinging to the hairs on my arms. My breath came out short. "What news?"

"You have a body in your morgue," Romero said gruffly. "A Mr. Charles Whitmore. I got off the phone with his mother this morning, and she has put in a request for it to be transferred to the city. For the funeral."

"Oh."

That was all I could say. For some reason, my brain stopped communicating with my mouth, rendering me speechless.

After appearing to be entirely mute, I finally gathered myself enough to ask, "When should I have him ready for the transfer?"

"Friday morning," the sheriff answered. "I know it's

short notice, but an influential family like the Whitmores move fast. And I do understand Mrs. Whitmore wanting her son home to be buried."

I tried to relax but failed miserably at it. "Of course. Sheriff—"

I stopped myself from mentioning the obituary or the other suspicious activity dotting Charles's past. The case was closed, and I doubted the sheriff would reopen it based on the hunch of a funeral home director and her quirky undertaker sidekicks. Without being able to pinpoint exactly what happened to Charles, or proving that he did, in fact, kill Greg Stollen, we had no proof.

The wind trilled over the cliffs, a haunting melody that seemed to echo from the depths of the gray, churning sea. Below, waves crashed in fierce, relentless strides against the jagged rocks, sending up sprays of mist that glistened like tiny ghosts in the dim, stormy light. I wrapped my housecoat tighter around myself, watching the sheriff's retreating form as he trudged back to his car, shoulders hunched against the biting cold.

The weight of the situation pressed down on me, heavy as the sky above. If we wanted justice for both men, it couldn't come a moment too soon. Friday morning was two nights away—a countdown already ticking in the back of my mind, each second pressing further down until I was ready to snap. Time was slipping through our fingers, and as the sheriff's car disappeared around the bend, I knew we were running out of it.

Chapter Twenty

This was, without a doubt, the least professional thing I'd done since I first opened the funeral home. Tucked behind a column and sitting on the floor, I watched in silent fascination as Mortimer, Rosemary, and Finn huddled over Charles Whitmore's body, each absorbed in their role. Mortimer, the most seasoned of the group, leaned in close, peering over his spectacles with a furrowed brow as he inspected the man's fingernails. Rosemary, in her usual meticulous manner, traced her gloved fingers along his arms, noting every blemish and bruise. Finn gently tilted Charles's head from side to side, examining his face from every possible angle. And Ellie, ever efficient, tapped away on her laptop, recording their every observation with rapid, precise strokes.

Despite all their efforts, none of us could pinpoint anything out of the ordinary. The original hospital's findings were backed by our own examinations so far. For all intents and purposes, Charles Whitmore had died of a heart attack, as the official report stated. There were no signs of foul play, no suspicious marks or unexplained injuries, nothing that would suggest he'd met with anything other than a natural, albeit sudden, end.

And yet, there was a nagging tension that we couldn't shake. We simply did not believe what was staring us right in the face.

I rested a hand on Theo's soft back and he purred in response. The cat insisted on following us to the morgue because, and I quote, this was way more interesting than Buffy the Vampire Slayer reruns. Colossal praise, since that was his favorite show.

"Is anyone going to do anything?" the cat whispered out of earshot of the others.

I frowned. "They are. They're looking for clues on the body."

"The body that literally everyone and their mother already checked? Wonderful."

Ignoring him, I drew my attention from the Wardens by the slab to Ellie. Her forehead was creased in concentration, and I saw that glint in her eyes that she had when she was close to figuring things out. It was the same expression she had on when she won the first clue point in the mausoleum.

My interest peaked.

I stood up and left Theo to his groans of disappointment—masked as meows—and walked over to the desk where Ellie worked. My neck craned to see over her shoulder. In front of her, the laptop screen lit up with a dozen different tabs. I watched the mortician zoom in on one paragraph in a medical examiner blog, then switch to a note app to relay the information.

Leaning in closer, I tried to make out what she typed, but she had already moved on to another website.

"Find anything?" I asked.

Ellie didn't turn around and kept scrolling through the website she was signed into. "Nothing groundbreaking. The only way Charles's heart could have given out was if he forgot to take his medication. But he'd have to skip too many doses for it to make a drastic difference, and even then, there would have to have been a trigger that made his heart stop abruptly."

"Hmm. What would be the chances that happened?"

"Slim to none," Ellie said. "The man has been on the stuff for years. No way he forgot to take his pills. It would have been a habit at this point for him."

"Like you forgetting to drink six cups of coffee in a day," Rosemary remarked from behind the slab.

Ellie's eyes flashed. "Which reminds me, I'm due for another. Mind if I use your kitchen really quick?"

When I nodded, she rolled the chair aside and rushed up the stairs, leaving an Ellie-shaped absence where she was a moment ago. I settled into her spot to continue the search while she was gone. No point missing a beat, since we were on a time crunch.

"She's going to overdose on caffeine if she doesn't curb that habit," Rosemary said softly.

My head jerked up at her words. A sinking feeling in my stomach made me shiver, and I locked eyes with Rosemary, my lips peeling back from my teeth. A tingling sensation ran through my body and my heart rate sped up. I stilled for a brief second.

Taking in a rapid, short breath, I looked from Rosemary to Mortimer and Finn. "Is it possible to take too much digitoxin?"

"What are you thinking?" Finn asked.

I worried my bottom lip, eyes flashing to the open laptop. "I'm not sure yet," I admitted. "Perhaps Charles didn't skip a dose of it, but took it twice, or more. Could that stop his heart somehow?"

Before anyone could answer, I added, "I'm thinking out loud here. It's probably nothing."

"No, no," Mortimer interjected. "Keep going. Are you saying that too much digitoxin in the body could have the opposite effect of what the medication is tailored to do?"

I sat back, my eyes narrowing as I sifted through a haze of half-formed thoughts, each one close but not quite reaching a solid foundation. My fingers drummed rhythmically on the edge of the desk. The idea slowly coming into clarity. The space between my eyebrows furrowed as I stared blankly at the notes Ellie typed out. Why was this specific theory nagging me so much? There was something here that I couldn't put my finger on.

It was as though the solution was hovering out of reach, a low hum in the back of my brain that I could almost hear.

I muttered under my breath, the Wardens watching me like I was a loose cannon about to go off. I could taste the answer on the tip of my tongue.

"Ouch!" I yelped.

I was so deep in thought that I bit that same tongue without realizing it. Suddenly, it happened. The pieces connected and the fog on my brain lifted. "Digitoxin..." I whispered. I got up, holding up a finger. "Be right back."

Following Ellie's previous exit, I bolted up the stairs, inconspicuously motioning for Theo to follow. For once, the cat didn't complain, and I heard his light footsteps padding behind me as I ran out of the morgue, taking the steps two at a time. When I reached the top landing, I made a sharp right and headed for the library. My feet slid across the polished wood floor and skidded to a stop in front of the shelf holding my gardening books.

I trailed a finger along the spines one by one.

"What's going on?" Theo asked. "You're acting certifiably out of your mind."

My hand curled around one book, and I yanked it out. "Aha! Got it!"

Moving quickly, I splayed the book open and flipped through the pages. When I found the section I was looking for, I crouched next to the cat and put the book down on the floor for him to see.

Theo's eyes widened in terror.

"Foxglove? Why, Lyra? What have I done to deserve such horrendous banishment?" he howled.

I waved him away. "It's not for you," I said. "I'd never expose you to a plant that's poisonous to you. But read this."

Pointing to a specific passage, I waited until Theo skimmed it. The cat's haunches rose, and he glared at me with his whiskers sticking straight out like little white antennas. I pursed my lips at him. Finally, he was on the same page.

"Foxglove is a source of digitoxin," Theo said. "If someone wanted to make Charles Whitmore overdose on his medication, they didn't need to force feed him more pills."

I let go of the breath I was holding in. "All they'd have to do is expose him to a flower. Who would suspect a flower?"

"No one. Unless you knew what you were looking for."

The blood in my veins boiled over as the realization smacked me straight in the face. If someone managed to get Charles to ingest Foxglove, it wouldn't get flagged on a tox report. The digitoxin in the flower wouldn't raise any red flag since Charles was already ingesting it for his heart. But there was a reason Foxglove used to be such a popular poison amongst the humans ages ago. When used correctly, it could kill someone without leaving a trace. At least not a trace that was easily recognizable.

I looked at the book between us, reading the effects of Foxglove poisoning on the human body. Gastrointestinal distress. Vision disturbances. Respiratory muscle paralysis. Rapid, erratic heartbeats. My eyes blurred as I reached the final one listed.

"*In severe poisoning cases, electrical signals may fail to transmit through the heart, stopping the heart entirely.*"

The cat shook out his fur. "Well, I'll be damned."

Every bone in my body turned to liquid. I fought

against the nausea settling in my gut, and forced my legs to move. Standing up shot a bout of vertigo into my brain, and I blinked rapidly, black dots swarming my vision. This was it. I knew it. Deep down, I was certain this was how Charles died. No. How someone *killed* him. Because there was no denying it any longer.

Charles Whitmore was murdered. And he was murdered for what he did nine years ago on that dark road in Fine Bay.

I tucked the book under my arm and bolted from the library. My legs pumped as I ran through the manor and back to the morgue. The others were going to lose it when they heard what I discovered. I landed on the bottom landing with a loud thump, loud enough to make everyone turn around to face me.

I counted the figures in the morgue. All four were here. Five, if you included Charles. Yet something wasn't right. Why were they all so pale? And why was everyone staring at me like I grew another head?

Panic laced through me. I patted my shoulder blades, but my wings were still under the illusion spell, so I wasn't freaking them out with my fae appearance.

Then what was going on?

I glanced at each of them in confusion. "What's happened?"

Finn was the first one to speak. He raised his arm, waving his cellphone in the air like a flag of surrender.

"The town sent out a state of emergency warning," he said. "The storm came early. Everyone is instructed to stay indoors until it passes. I hope you wanted company because none of us are leaving any time soon."

My chest collapsed. For the love of fairy wings. Could nothing ever go right around here?

Chapter Twenty-One

The kettle screamed bloody murder, its shrill whistle cutting through the heavy silence of the kitchen. Steam billowed from its spout, curling upward in ghostly tendrils and fogging up the glossy subway tile of the backsplash. I flicked the burner off, carefully pouring the boiling water into the largest teapot I owned—a sturdy ceramic piece painted with bright sunflowers. The teapot gave a satisfying clink as I set it down. Five mismatched cups waited in a neat line on the counter, their faded patterns mocking me with years of use. I inherited the set with the house and was yet to replace it.

The tea would take a few minutes to steep, during which I leaned against the counter, rubbing my hands together for warmth.

The storm had raged for hours now, thick flakes of snow piling against the windowpanes and frosting the edges with crystalline patterns. Outside, the world was a monochrome blur; the landscape consumed by a relentless blanket of white. I peered through the kitchen window, narrowing my eyes in an attempt to make out the familiar silhouette of the cliffs in the distance. They were almost obscured, barely visible through the swirling storm. Only the faintest glimpses of deep red interrupted the blank expanse—rose petals peering out like drops of blood in the snow.

My poor babies. Even from here, I could sense their struggle, the way they reached for sunlight that wasn't coming anytime soon. A pang of guilt nudged at me for not covering them better before the storm hit. But then, who could have predicted this weather would last so long?

I made a note to siphon extra magic into the flowers around the property once it stopped snowing, to make up for this dreadful weather. Hopefully, there wouldn't be much damage, but at this point, I was glad I could still open the front door without being drowned in snow.

Behind me, muffled laughter and voices drifted from the living room where the rest of our impromptu sleepover crew was camped out. With the storm refusing to let up, it looked like I'd be hosting the Wardens for a while yet. A flicker of unease rippled through me—what if it got worse?

I turned back to the teapot, its sides now warm to the touch, and grabbed the tray. If we were going to be stuck here, we might as well have some tea to keep us warm. The Wardens had made themselves comfortable in there while we waited out the storm and we had spent the last few hours brainstorming as to who may have poisoned Charles Whitmore.

We hadn't gotten very far.

The internet connection was spotty because of all the wind interference, and there was little online about Greg Stollen's hit-and-run anyhow. Besides, the police got nowhere finding out who killed the man back in the day, and I doubted we'd have better luck. Especially since we were stuck indoors.

The tray wiggled, and the cups clanked against each other as I set it down on the coffee table. On the floor, Ellie and Rosemary stretched their legs. Piles of books from my library lay open around them.

I looked at the women quizzically. "You know, if you have any gardening questions, I'm happy to answer," I suggested. "You don't have to sift through every book on the shelf."

"Where did you learn that much about it?" Rosemary asked.

I bristled. "My mother was brilliant in the garden.

She had a real...green thumb," I said, masking the truth of my heritage. "When I left home and set up shop here in Orchard Hollow, it was the first thing I did. The flowers remind me of her."

"Have you gone back home since?" Finn asked.

I glanced at him over my shoulder. "It's not that simple, I'm afraid."

If Finn wished to ask me more, he held his tongue. Instead, he picked up a cup and took a long sip. His lips twitched.

"I thought you weren't a tea drinker," I noted.

Finn shrugged, taking one more sip. His gaze met mine. "It's growing on me."

Was it me, or was it hotter than the Summer Court in August in here? The atmosphere was stifling, thick with tension, but nothing compared to the look Finn was giving me. It wasn't just a glance—it was a slow, deliberate gaze that seemed to peel back every layer of my composure. Every molecule in my body combusted under it, leaving me hot and flustered despite my best efforts to appear nonchalant. My face burned, and I was pretty sure I'd turned the exact shade of the roses blooming in the garden outside.

Desperate for a distraction, I reached for the nearest cup of tea, a poorly thought-out decision I regretted the instant my hands touched the fine china. The heat seared through my palms with the force of a thousand suns. I bit down hard on the inside of my cheek to stifle a yelp, my lips pressed into a tight line as I fought the urge to drop the cup entirely.

With no concern for elegance or grace, I hastily set the cup down on the fireplace mantel. The movement was rushed, clumsy, and tea sloshed over the rim, splattering onto the floor below. My eyes darted to Finn, silently hoping he hadn't noticed—or worse, found amusement in my complete lack of decorum.

He was still watching me.

Fairy help me.

Around us, the Wardens busied themselves with conversation, completely oblivious to the circus before them. The only true relief was that no one saw me make a fool of myself. Perhaps I was overreacting and Finn wasn't showing any interest in me at all. I averted my gaze. Whether he was or wasn't didn't matter.

I couldn't risk getting involved with anyone. It wasn't safe. Not until I was absolutely certain my egomaniac ex-fiancé wouldn't come knocking.

The muffled sound of voices broke through my mental self-flagellation. "Orchard Hollow really needs to keep better records of people who die here," I heard Rosemary say.

"In their defense," Mortimer argued, "Mr. Stollen didn't die here. Maybe once the storm lets up, we can go to Fine Bay and see what we can dig up there."

"Pun intended?" Ellie asked.

Mortimer smirked. "Always."

A sudden realization anchored my feet in place. I froze, my mind latching onto what Rosemary said. My lips trembled ever so slightly when I asked, "What did you say?"

"The part about going to Fine Bay to sleuth around?" Mortimer asked.

I brushed him off. "No, I meant Rosemary. You mentioned records of the dead in Orchard Hollow."

"Um, sure, yes. I said it would have been lovely to have that."

Tearing my attention from her, I looked at Finn. "But we have that already, don't we?"

"You're not proposing we speak to the librarian," Finn said.

"I definitely am!" I said excitedly. "Who else would know about some random hit-and-run a few towns over other than Maggie Halloway? You said it yourself: the woman is writing a book about unexplained deaths in Orchard Hollow. How much do you want to bet that she'd have at least *some* information on what happened to Greg Stollen? Because I'm willing to wager it's a lot more than the police have." When no one said anything, I added, "One thing I learned while living here is that when it comes to small towns, gossip travels faster than police reports."

Mortimer stood up before I could make a transcendent case for why my idea was brilliant enough to try. He walked out of the room, his feet shuffling down the hall and toward the front foyer. The four of us exchanged wordless glances. I opened my mouth to ask where he went, but Finn held up a finger, pointing to the open living door.

Less than a minute later, Mortimer walked back inside, a phone pressed to his ear. I tried not to laugh that the cellphone was possibly the first one to have ever been invented—as ancient as Mortimer himself. It flipped, for Fairy's sake. Did phones do that anymore?

Surely this was a prototype from the nineties.

Mortimer's lips twitched into a grin as he lowered to sit down.

"Yes, yes, I'm still here, Maggie. Apologies, these lines tend to crackle fiercely... Now, you were saying about the...hit-and-run? Mmm. Yes, tragic business, that. Left his poor family with no answers, not even a proper witness to speak of."

He paused, leaning back in his chair, his voice carefully calm, though there was a note of curiosity when he spoke to the librarian. I hadn't realized they were friends. Though, didn't Finn say that anyone who dealt with the dead knew of the librarian? It would make sense that Mortimer and she crossed professional paths. And yet his tone was not exactly detached. If I had to guess, I'd say our Warden had a past with Maggie Halloway. One I wanted to know more about later.

"Ah, a fiancée, you say? Here, in Orchard Hollow? A florist, no less. My, my. That does add a rather poignant detail, doesn't it?"

The floorboards beneath me creaked, but Mortimer didn't seem to visit. Sweat beaded on my lower back. Did he say florist?

"She never came forward? Strange...I would have thought such a connection would come to light, even in a town this small. People do have a way of talking."

Mortimer took out a pen from the breast pocket of his suit and jotted words down on one of the paper napkins I brought with the tea. He tapped the pen against chin as he said, "Yes, Maggie, I quite agree. It makes one wonder if there was more to this story than meets the eye. Secrets buried, as it were. Oh, forgive the phrasing."

He paused briefly, his tone shifting to panic.

"No, no. I don't mean to pry into your book—though I confess, it sounds fascinating. But the florist...does she still live here? Yes? I see. Maggie, if you don't mind my asking, has she ever spoken to you of this? About him? Ah, I see. Flowers left at his grave, you say. Quite touching. And yet, no public acknowledgment..."

Outside, the wind knocked something over, and a loud crack sounded through the house. Mortimer straightened his back. He paused again, his lips pressing together as he listened. I held my breath.

"A Miss Daisy Rivers, you say. Much obliged. You've been most helpful. And Maggie? Do let me know about next weekend. I'm itching to win a poker hand for a change."

He chuckled lightly, then said goodbye and hung up the phone. When he turned to us, the group bombarded him with questions.

"How do you know the librarian?"

"Why didn't you mention this sooner?"

"What poker game? Can I come?"

Everyone needed an answer so desperately you could feel it in the air around us. I was the only one who had her mouth buttoned up shut. The thing was, I didn't care how Mortimer knew the librarian, nor did I care to join their poker game, which was obviously a date. What I cared about most was that I heard the name he pried from the woman on the phone. It was the same florist Maggie Halloway recommended when she came around here looking for answers about Charles.

Acid filled my throat, choking me.

A florist would most definitely have access to Foxglove. But Daisy Rivers had more than that, didn't she? She had the motive to want Charles dead.

Chapter Twenty-Two

"Daisy Rivers first rented the shop on Dandelion Lane eight-and-a-half years ago," Rosemary said. She clicked a button, and the printer I dragged in from the morgue's office whirred to life. It spat out a piece of paper with the store hours of the Petal and Thorn flower shop, alongside a map of its location. Rosemary put it on the floor next to the other papers we'd collected. "Almost a year after her fiancé died."

"Why here?" Finn asked.

I wholeheartedly agreed with him. "Why not Fine Bay where she lived?"

A recollection of my chat with the librarian came to mind. I paused.

"I believe she has a cousin in the area," I said. "But it still doesn't explain why she'd uproot her life to start a business that far from her home."

There was a rustle as Rosemary sifted through our pile of online sleuthing, tossing papers aside when they didn't have what she was searching for. The rest of us waited with bated breath. Well, three of us. Mortimer was too busy scratching behind Theo's ears, who played the part of a real cat with such precision I would have mistaken him for one myself if I didn't know better.

I cocked my head to the side when he purred louder than my old vacuum. Everything about this situation made me uneasy.

Forcing my eyes away from the bizarre pairing on the couch, I turned back to Rosemary, who finally found whatever it was she needed. She put three pages side by side, her knowing eyes glistening.

"This is the first news article announcing Whitmore Industries moving in on Orchard Hollow land," she said. "Three years after Greg's accident."

"Are you suggesting that she specifically chose Orchard Hollow to...what? Run into Charles Whitmore on the off chance he came to town? How would she even get access to him long enough to poison him?"

Rosemary shook her head. She pointed to the second page she had laid out earlier. "That's not really what I'm thinking of. Five years ago, the Whitmores built a condominium complex in Fine Bay. Right by the water," she said. "Guess who bought a one-bedroom condo in it with the money she inherited from her fiancé's insurance claim?"

I snatched the paper and read over the small text. My eyes rounded.

"Daisy lived in a condo built by Whitmore Industries," I whispered. "Do you think she knew the man who killed her fiancé and got away with it owned the place?"

"No, but I think she may have figured it out while living there."

We exchanged glances that were somewhere between doubtful and intrigued.

"Okay, hear me out," Rosemary said. "Say she bought a place and was finally starting her life over after mourning Greg. She goes about her days completely unaware that the man who killed him is actually kind of her landlord. Then one day, she sees Charles and the pieces click into place. She goes to the police, but no one believes her since she has no proof. So she decides to take matters into her own hands. She sees that Charles is planning to build here in town and formulates a plan for revenge."

Ellie harrumphed from her corner of the living

room, tucked between two large pillows. "How would she know who Charles is, to recognize him in the first place?"

In response, Rosemary pulled up the third piece of paper she found.

"Because she was staying at the Rose Hollow Hotel on the night Greg died," she said, showing us a printed photo of Daisy Rivers pulled from a social media site. In it, Daisy beamed in a wide smile, posing for the camera in front of the hotel's bronze doors. "She and Charles were in the same place at the same time. She might have seen him there."

"I don't know," Finn said. "It's a lot of assumptions. If this is what happened, why a flower shop? Why wouldn't she just shoot the guy?"

Rosemary puffed out her full lips. "I'm not certain. There has to be a reason and a connection, but I'm not seeing it here."

Outside, the storm rattled the windows, and we watched snow fall in clumps from the roof. A few more hours of this and we would be buried under it. I had already made peace with the fact that the Wardens might be staying until tomorrow, and had begun to prepare the guest rooms for each of them. The beauty of living in an old manor was one was never short on rooms. I could probably open my own bed-and-breakfast if the whole undertaker thing didn't work out.

I chuckled under my breath. Whom was I kidding? It was a miracle I wasn't breaking out in hives having the Wardens here. I could never handle so many strangers traipsing through. My gaze flicked to Theo. Besides, when would the changeling be himself, if there were humans around all the time?

A deafening creak tore me from my thoughts. My head swiveled back to the window, where I watched in astonishment as one of the trees lining the driveway bent unnaturally from the wind. Its trunk strained so hard it might have snapped, were it not for the thick oak beside it holding it steady.

My heart sank to my toes.

If we had any shot of finding out the truth about Daisy and Charles, we had to do it before this storm took over the town.

I pulled out my phone and pulled up the funeral home's e-mail. Typing quickly, I put together a message that would work and pressed *send*. Then I waited. It took only ten minutes for a reply to arrive.

I smirked, a wolf in sheep's clothing.

"Would you all mind holding down the fort?" I asked the Wardens.

"Um, why? Where are you going?"

I rolled my shoulders back, my spine snapping. "I only now realized that I did not have time to make arrangements for flowers for a visitation Friday afternoon."

"Absolutely not," Finn said sternly. "You are not going to see that woman. Especially not in this weather."

"It's the only way we can get the answers we need."

Next to him, Rosemary placed a hand on Finn's arm to keep him calm. "The flower shop is likely closed because of the storm," she said.

"It's not," I replied. "I checked. Daisy said if I can get there in the next twenty minutes, she'll help me out. So I need to be quick."

As I started for the door, the scraping of chair legs on hardwood made me pause. Heavy footsteps thundered behind me, and when I turned, I saw Finn's towering figure at my back. I grimaced. "What are you doing?"

"If you think I'm letting you go alone, you're sorely mistaken."

My temples throbbed. Was there any point arguing with the man? By the look of him, I had a better chance of convincing Theo to give Mortimer a break from petting him than getting Finn to back down. My eyes drifted to the clock. Time was literally ticking away.

The sound of the minute hand switching made my knees knock.

"Fine," I told Finn. "But I'm driving."

"Because it's your plan?"

I rolled my eyes. "Because your car got buried under four feet of snow thirty minutes ago," I said. "And my truck is right there."

With that, I turned on my heel and marched to the front door, not bothering to check if he was behind me.

Chapter Twenty-Three

Tires slid and swerved as I maneuvered the truck around unplowed roads. We avoided the cliff-side drive, a shorter route to the flower shop, but one that was much too dangerous in these conditions, and opted for small residential streets. On either side, windows lit up houses from within and chimneys pumped out smoke and steam. All of Orchard Hollow was hiding indoors to wait out the storm. All but Finn and me.

I shifted gears to climb a steep hill, then shifted again as we went sliding down the other side of it. The truck skidded at the base, and it took all my strength to correct its trajectory and avoid the gargantuan snow pile on our right.

Maybe I should have let Finn drive. Not that I

couldn't manage it, but at least if we did get into an accident, I wouldn't feel as guilty about dragging him out here. Though he didn't exactly give me another option.

I side-eyed him in the passenger seat. What was his game here?

"It should be past those lights," Finn said, pointing to the red light ahead of us.

I pulled to a slow rolling stop and unclenched my white-knuckling hands from the wheel. "Good," I said. I looked at the emptied-out streets around us. "Parking won't be an issue."

Finn barreled out a hearty laugh. "Way to look on the bright side. Let's get this over with fast so we don't get snowed-in with a possible killer."

"*Possible* is the key word here," I said as I made the turn. "We don't know if anything Rosemary said about the fiancée is true. For all we know, we are going in there on pure speculation."

I swerved to avoid an uprooted tree lying in the middle of the road. The tires squealed as the truck ripped around the side and climbed onto the sidewalk. Stepping off the gas, I moved it back to the road and made the final turn that took us to Dandelion Lane. Next to me, Finn held onto the overhead bar like it was the last parachute on a plane going down fast.

"Glad to hear we're risking our lives on sheer speculation."

Ignoring him, I parked the truck halfway on the curb and climbed out. The wind knocked me from side to side, and I had to grip the cold metal of the car to keep from falling flat on my butt. My hair swirled over my face, and my cheeks burned from the icy blasts that attacked my skin. I hurried over to Finn, using his wide frame to shield myself from the elements ever so slightly. Huddling close together, we made our way toward Petal and Thorn. My heart stopped for a second as the flower shop came into view.

The flower shop stood out sorely against the swirling chaos of the snowstorm. Its painted wooden sign, showing three roses in a bunch, creaked slightly on its iron hinges as windblown snowflakes clung to its edges. Frost edged the corners of the wide front windows, but the golden glow of lights from inside spilled onto the snow-covered sidewalk. Within the shop, bouquets of roses, daisies, and lilies displayed in buckets adorned the ledges of both window openings.

A chalkboard propped outside the door, half-buried under a growing drift, announced in looping handwriting, *"Fresh Blooms for Fresh Souls!"* Icicles hung from the awning, catching the light of a string of twinkling fairy lights that framed the storefront. The glass door, its brass handle polished to a shiny perfection, was the only thing in the front that wasn't covered by the storm.

If it wasn't for the possible murderer inside, the place was truly magical.

Finn opened the door and held it for me to walk in. I could see his muscles strain as he fought against the frigid current outside that wanted to rip the door from his grip and slam it shut. Above our heads, the little bell that welcomed visitors rang incessantly until we scurried indoors and closed the door behind us.

The interior of the flower shop was as adorable as the snowed-in windows implied. I felt like I was stepping into a floral wonderland. My chest swelled with emotion at the sight of the flowers blooming all around me. Marigolds. Irises. Dahlias. The shop had the most interesting selection I'd seen in a while. The scent of fresh blooms mingled with damp soil, a comfortable combination I loved from years spent in a garden. Rows of wooden shelves, painted a soft yellow, were lined with pots of ferns, succulents, and other greenery, their leaves glistening faintly with droplets from a recent misting.

The same buckets as we saw in the windows filled the interior of the shop, each full of vibrant flowers that stood on weathered wooden crates. The buckets were sorted by color and type, creating a gorgeous mix of reds, yellows, pinks, and blues that battled against the dreariness outside.

A long counter at the back of the shop served as the

workspace, cluttered with spools of satin ribbon, sharp shears, and rolls of craft paper.

In one corner, a small seating area with a metal chair and a low table held a steaming teapot. This place was truly after my own heart.

"Lyra Moore?" a woman's voice asked from behind a wall of lilies.

I stretched my neck to see her, my spine steeling. Daisy Rivers was not what I expected. Standing at no more than five feet tall, she was almost entirely obscured by the towering flowers surrounding her. Her brown hair fell in effortless waves down her back, and she wore a summer-patterned dress that clashed with the wretched winter outside. With her rosy cheeks and rosier complexion, she reminded more of a fairy than a human woman. My nose twitched as I sniffed for magic.

Confirming that Daisy wasn't one of my kind, I let my guard drop a little. Which was more than I could say for Finn, whose eyes were so narrowed I wondered if he could see anything at all.

I jabbed him in the ribs, then extended a warm smile in Daisy's direction. "That's me," I said. "Thank you so much for staying open for us."

"No problem. I was locking up and around anyhow," Daisy said. "You mentioned arrangements for a visitation?"

I nodded in agreement. "Yes, that's right. You have

some beautiful options. I wish I knew about your place sooner."

"Thank you," Daisy replied with a blush. "Always nice to meet another person who appreciates flowers."

"Is that why you became a florist?" Finn asked.

Daisy shook her head. "Not really. I have always loved the idea, but believe it or not, I was in pharmaceuticals in a past life."

Keeping my gaze on the woman, I worked not to look at Finn. I was pretty certain he was thinking the same thing I was, and I didn't want to spook Daisy quite yet. Someone who worked with drugs would definitely know their way around poisons.

I swung my head around the shop but didn't see any Foxglove plants. Not that I expected Daisy to have the murder weapon out in the open, and it wasn't like the flower was in high demand by the general public. My eyes darted to the door behind her. A back room, perhaps. I wondered if that was where Daisy kept the plant, if our theory was right and she did use it to poison Charles.

"Why did you decide to open a flower shop?" I asked. "It's a big change from pharmaceuticals."

"I had my reasons," Daisy said. "Why don't you take a look around and see what you like? I have pre-made arrangements to the left." She glanced out the front window. "It's likely better to go with those, to give yourselves time to get back before the worst of it hits."

I pulled Finn toward the low shelf holding said arrangements and turned my back to Daisy. The woman busied herself with putting things away, giving us a moment alone and out of earshot. Sliding in closer to Finn, I kept my voice low when I asked, "What do you think?"

"I'm not sure," he answered. "She seems to be the right fit, but I can't picture it."

"Me too. She seems too...I don't know...cheerful. I'm not getting any hints of a woman in mourning...definitely not someone who's angry enough to kill for revenge."

A muscle feathered in Finn's jaw. "It's possible we made a mistake. We should get what you need and head back."

"Would you two like some tea for the road?" Daisy yelled out from behind us. "I put a fresh pot on before you got here to stay warm."

I looked up at Finn, and when he nodded, said, "Sure. Why not?"

We can use the excuse to question you more, anyhow.

The smell of bergamot and mint drifted toward me and my entire body pulled toward the tea as though it were magnetized. Deep down, I was really hoping we were right, and Daisy was not the killer, because she was exactly the kind of person I wanted to be around. Loved flowers? Check. Brewed an excellent tea? Check.

What else did one need in a friend?

I skipped toward her extended hand and snatched the steaming cup, taking a long, magical sip. My shoulders slumped. Next to me, Finn wasn't as overjoyed as I was, but he still drank the delicious concoction, and I did see him grin a little, which was a huge sign of improvement. It's possible I was growing on the guy after all.

I sucked in an inhale, stopping short when another scent overwhelmed my sharp senses. Was that lilac? Glancing around the shop, I didn't see any, so it was strange to be able to smell it. The hairs on my arms stood up, electrified. It was the same scent I smelled at the cemetery when I thought I was being followed.

"What perfume are you wearing?" I asked Daisy.

Her lips twitched. "Lilacs in Bloom," she said. "It was my fiancé's favorite. He used to gift it to me each birthday; had to order it months in advance from overseas, since they didn't sell it here. Do you like it?"

"I-I..." The words would not come. I had them, only I couldn't say them. My lips have stopped working from some sort of paralysis.

"A little early this time," Daisy said. She took the teacup from me before I dropped it to the floor, because much like my mouth, my hands have also frozen.

Walking past me, she grabbed Finn's cup from him, the scent of lilacs washing over both of us as she passed. The flower shop owner looked from Finn's terrified face to mine. "Sorry about this. Truly."

I tried to reach for her, but my hands were as useless as the rest of me. My stomach turned, bile coating it as it began to spasm. The realization of what was happening made my head pound. Tears swelled behind my widening eyes. I was wrong. I wasn't paralyzed.

Daisy poisoned the tea with Foxglove, and by the look of what was happening, it was a high enough dose to kill. A tremor shook my body. I tried to scream, but no sound came out. Black swarmed my vision and the blood in my veins felt like it was reaching its boiling point. The last thing I saw before darkness took me was Finn crashing to the floor beside me.

Chapter Twenty-Four

The world spun around me, my bones feeling like water in oil inside my body. I struggled to open my eyes, but there was no use fighting it. The Foxglove in my system made it impossible to think clearly. A heavy fog settled over my brain that I couldn't lift. If I was in my right mind, I would have realized how close the sensation was to stepping through a portal. Actually, now that I thought of it, a rancid panic shot through me.

Did I imagine coming to the flower shop? Was this some trick of the fae?

My heart raced in my aching chest.

I couldn't go back to Fairy. No matter what, I had to fight for my freedom and my life.

Wait, that wasn't right. Something was wrong, and it

wasn't me being dragged back to Fairy. I tried to think back to the last ten minutes, but nothing came to mind. Wasn't I thinking about Foxglove? The flower was important. Why?

My head spun as I attempted to work out the horrid mess in my mind. Flashes of driving in the snow danced before me, and I clung to the memories like a vulture. I wasn't alone in the car. Someone was with me. Who?

A sharp pain in my gut made me scream internally. Suddenly, a moment of clarity appeared, and I saw Finn sitting in the passenger seat, his hand clutching the overhead handle for dear life as I swerved around a fallen tree. The memories of the last half hour rushed through my system, overwhelming me with their presence. I wanted to throw up, but my body refused to move. All I saw was black, though that was probably because my eyes were closed. An image of Daisy's face made my blood boil.

That horrible woman tried to poison me! And Finn!

Terror laced through my bones as I thought about the morgue director. He drank her death tea as well and chances were that he was much further along than I was. My fae blood slowed the effects of the poison, a thing Daisy didn't account for since she was human and wasn't aware of the supernaturals in her quaint little town. Well, guess what, Daisy? I wasn't about to go down so easily.

With the last of my waning strength, I tapped into my fairy magic and let it surge through every nerve in my body. The energy was warm and electric, crackling like a storm contained beneath my skin, and I guided it with precision. Sparks flooded my brain, sharpening my thoughts as I turned inward, seeking out the poison that had dulled my senses. My magic flowed like a tide, wrapping around every remnant of the toxin, encasing it in a shimmering barrier of light. The connection I felt with the natural world deepened as I worked—my magic wasn't a force, but an extension of nature itself—it was the core of my very being.

Fairies were not like humans when it came to poisons. Certain flowers, such as Foxglove, could wreak havoc on our systems, clouding our minds and dragging us into lethargy, but they could not destroy us. Instead, it felt like fighting off a shadow of ourselves, for we shared the same essence as the plants that grew wild and untamed. We were as much a part of nature as the Foxglove was. By surrounding the poison with magic, I wasn't simply purging it. I was reminding it of its place, harmonizing with the energy that had sought to kill me.

To put it plainly, whatever Daisy tried to do, it wouldn't work on me.

My lids felt glued together as I peeled them open one by one, to find myself lying on my side on the floor of the flower shop. Strings of lights hanging on the ceiling blended into one as my vision reformed and sharpened. I blinked, the motion sending cascading needles down my cheeks. I could hear Daisy mumble to herself near to me, but she wasn't close enough to see. Doing my best not to alert her to me waking up, I rolled over and searched for Finn.

Unlike me, he wasn't in the same spot he had dropped down in.

It appeared that Daisy had moved him while he was unconscious. I saw a glimpse of his ridiculous newspaper-boy hat peeking out from behind the counter. My breath caught when I realized that I couldn't see if he was breathing from this vantage point. My mind raced.

I needed to get to Finn to check if he was alive, and I needed to do it without Daisy noticing.

Slowly, I raised my head and looked around the shop. There was no sign of her, but I could hear her light voice drifting in from somewhere close. My gaze landed on the door I saw before. It was cracked open, and a light streamed in from the opening, Daisy's voice muffled on the other side.

I rose on my elbow and dragged myself over to the cluttered flower arrangement counter and closer to Finn. Every inch was agonizing as my body fought against the poison, returning to what it was before. Sweat pooled on my forehead and fell into my eyes, blinding me temporarily. I rubbed at them until my skin felt raw and angry, and kept going. When I reached him, I all but collapsed on his chest.

Which was, thankfully, still moving up and down.

I pressed two fingers to the inside of his wrist and felt for a pulse. Relief flooded through me when I felt the thumping of it. It was faint, but it was there. For now.

Finn's skin was ashen and his lips were an unnatural color. He wouldn't last long unless I could get some medical help here immediately. I racked my brain for something I could do in the meantime and came up empty. No amount of magic could help me here. Finn was human, and I was not a strong enough fairy to interfere or alter the harm done to his body. Besides, my specialty wasn't even in the same wheelhouse as the type of magic this might have required.

Anxiety shredded me to pieces. If I wanted him to live, I had to get rid of Daisy long enough to call for an ambulance.

My magic tingled under my skin as I rose on rubbery legs and made my way toward the back room of the flower shop. Using every surface available to me for support, I crept closer to the light streaming from the opening. Daisy's voice had gone quiet since I checked on Finn and worry ate away at me. *What if she's gone?* She could have easily left us to die here with plans to return after the storm passed. It wouldn't be so bad, except I was pretty sure that if she left, she'd have locked the place up...and us in it. And what did I plan to do when I confronted her?

A few sparkly zaps tangled between my fingers. I didn't have a choice. I had to use my fairy magic, even if it meant that Daisy would find out what I was. Maybe there would be a chance to work it out later, but right now, it was the only option I had.

My magic was Finn's only hope of living through the night.

Straightening my shoulders, I gathered myself together and pushed the door open. For a moment, I thought I had been right—that Daisy did abandon us to our doom and the storm's ravaging. Then I saw her standing in between two large potted palms, her hands worrying over a rope she was trying to untie. I scanned the narrow back room of the shop while Daisy's back was turned. The space was filled with boxes, and empty pottery, and several tools I recognized as the same ones I used in my garden back at the manor. To my right, a heavy-set metal door rattled from the wind. I relaxed my stance. There was another way out should I need to think quickly and escape.

My hands reached for a pair of large shears that appeared sharp enough to serve as a weapon to protect myself with. Without making a sound, I held them up, pointy sides forward, and approached Daisy. My feet padded so softly that she didn't register me standing right behind her.

I opened my mouth with a plan to scare her enough to drop her guard, but my words were cut off by a horrifying click and the pressing of a cold, metal object to the rear of my head. I swallowed the growing lump in my throat.

"Turn around slowly," a gruff male voice said.

I did as I was told. Even before I turned, I knew what that sound was. Someone else was here with us, someone with a gun.

Blood drained from my face as I saw who was standing before me. I licked my cracked lips, my gaze stone-cold. "You?"

Chapter Twenty-Five

rthur Malone glared at me down the barrel of a shiny silver gun. It seemed impossibly large, a dark, unblinking eye that stared back at me with complete indifference. The gun wavered slightly, its movements mirroring the tremor in Arthur's hand. The air between us was so heavy it felt like a physical force pressing against my chest. As if Arthur's gun was touching my body and not a few feet away.

I couldn't tear my gaze away, my breath hitching in uneven gasps. Every nerve in my body screamed to run, but my legs were locked, frozen in place. My heart pounded so hard it felt as though it might burst, the sound filling my ears and drowning out everything else. A bead of sweat slid down my temple, its slow path making me crawl out of my skin. Fear clawed at my throat and made it difficult to swallow the saliva collecting under my tongue.

Before me, Arthur shifted his stance, and the motion sent a fresh wave of panic through me. His knuckles were pale where they gripped the weapon, tendons taut, and fingers curled tightly as if the gun might leap from his hand if he let up for even a second. His eyes burned with something that was hard to define—anger, desperation, maybe fear of his own. It made him seem unsteady and unpredictable. Dangerous. Not like the man I recalled from the diner one bit.

"Don't move," he growled.

I wasn't sure why he needed to include the extra instruction—I wasn't going anywhere.

"Is that really necessary?" Daisy asked from behind me.

She skirted around me slowly, coming to stand by Arthur. So that was who she was talking to back here when I thought she was mumbling to herself. Now that they stood side by side, a switch clicked on in my head. The resemblance between them was uncanny. Daisy had the same crooked nose Arthur had, and their eyes were an identical shade of green, though Daisy's were larger and somewhat more innocent in appearance. I traced their features with my gaze carefully.

"You two are related, aren't you?"

Arthur bristled, and the gun wavered again. "I thought you'd have figured that out the second you walked in here," he said. "Daisy is my cousin. On my mother's side."

My stomach tensed. Arthur was the cousin the librarian mentioned Daisy had in town. And she was the one calling him in the diner upon our first meeting. My mind spun in tight circles. *The family that kills together...* Eyes darting between them, I tried to appear less horrified than I currently felt, but every few seconds flashes of Finn's poisoned body ran through my head, and I was back to square one. How was I going to get out of this one? The plan was great until there were two people to handle. And now that they both knew I was alive and well, the element of surprise was gone. Not to mention the gun pointed at my heart that I was certain was not a fake.

"I thought you said she drank the tea?" Arthur asked his cousin.

Daisy harrumphed. "She did! I have no idea how she's even walking around right now?" She looked at me skeptically. "It should have worked."

"Like it worked on Charles?" I asked.

"Charles Whitmore deserved every agonizing second he received," Arthur hissed out. His hand tightened around the gun's grip. "He deserved more. You didn't know him like I did. The things he did for money were despicable, and the world is a better place without him in it."

I narrowed my eyes at him. "Why work for a man you clearly despised? If you hated Charles so deeply, why did you stay on as his family's real estate agent?"

"I wasn't planning on being in his employ for this long. As a matter of fact, I had planned on quitting in that same month I got the call from Daisy telling me what Charles did to Greg. How that disgusting family covered it all up, tossed justice for Greg in the trash like he was roadkill."

That tracked. Since Arthur was the Whitmore's agent here in town, it made sense his cousin would call the second she figured out what happened to her fiancé. I wondered if they came up with their plan to take him down then, or if they sat on it for a while before committing. Mostly, I wondered how two people could go to such extremes to kill someone. Charles may have been a horrible person and a killer, yet what did that say about these two? They were willing to kill me and Finn to get away with their crime.

My face twisted into a scowl. "You spent years planning this out," I whispered. "Why not take it to the police?"

"Ha!" Daisy barked out. "You don't think we tried? I told the cops exactly what I suspected, and they wrote it off. Sent me away as some hysterical woman who was mourning. No one cared to hear the truth, and even if they did, it wouldn't do any good. The Whitmores had deep pockets. I doubted anything would come of it in the end."

"So you took it into your own hands."

Both nodded, glancing at each other.

"It was Arthur's idea," Daisy said. She smiled, and it made acid rise in my throat. "A brilliant plan, really. No one would suspect a man that had heart troubles dying, especially one that had such a stressful life. And thanks to the medication he was on, it was so easy to go through with. All we had to do was get him to drink the Foxglove tea."

My tongue swelled in my mouth. "That was why he came into town," I said to Arthur. "You told him to meet you here. The deal with the Whistling Kettle was a ploy to get Charles to show up so you could poison him. And he wouldn't say *no* to his trusted real estate agent. All you had to do was get him alone and give him the tea to drink."

"Yes, it was an excellent plan. Until you figured it out," Daisy said.

"When did you realize it?" I asked. "I know it was you at the cemetery. I could smell your perfume."

For a moment, Daisy startled, her bright green eyes widening as if she'd been caught off guard. She took an instinctive step back, her polished boots scuffing against the tiled floor. She buckled slightly as though the weight of my words had tipped her off balance. Her expression flickered—surprise melting into wariness—as if she were trying to piece together a puzzle, she hadn't realized she was part of. Was I simply perceptive, unusually attuned to my surroundings, or was there something more at play?

Her brows furrowed, and I could practically see the gears turning in her mind. No one would ever assume a fae was among them. The confusion rippled across her features, leaving her gaze guarded.

She placed a hand on Arthur's shoulder. "She knows too much. They both do."

"I'm sorry," the agent said softly. "I really am."

Then he fired the gun.

The next few things happened all at once. The bullet shot toward me at an unbearable speed, leaving no room for me to think. I threw my hands up and my magic exploded from my fingers right as it reached me. Sparks of light and fairy magic burst around me, creating a shield of protection over my body. The bullet bounced off and ricocheted into the back wall. As it zoomed past Daisy and Arthur, I saw the shop owner's eyes bulge in shock.

Before they could react, the back door burst open and blinding lights swirled over us. Shouts rose through the rear of the flower shop as the sheriff and two officers rushed inside. The officers moved in on Arthur, taking away his weapon and cuffing his hands behind his back. At the same time, the sheriff followed suit with Daisy, who had begun to cry as soon as the metal wrapped around her wrists.

Sheriff Romero was not remotely moved by her wails. He tightened the cuffs and handed her off to one of the officers to be led outside, where I assumed she'd be deposited into the back of a cruiser car alongside her murderous cousin.

"No! You have to stop her!" Daisy yelled as she was escorted out. "She's not human!"

Chills racked my body from her words. The sheriff locked eyes with me. For a second, I thought I saw a hint of understanding behind his serious gaze. With slow steps, he sauntered over to me, tipping his hat. "Miss Moore," he said. "Is Finn O'Malley here with you?"

"Oh. Y-yes," I stuttered out. "He needs help. Daisy and Arthur poisoned him, and I don't know how long he'll last. It was Foxglove."

"I am already aware. The paramedics are out front and ready to take him to the hospital immediately."

I curled my arms over my chest, shaking. "How did you know to come?"

"I got a call from a Mortimer Graves," the sheriff replied. "He was adamant that you were in danger.

Filled us in on the situation with Daisy, and made sure that we came all guns blazing. You're lucky to be alive."

I nodded. "Very lucky."

The sheriff looked between me and the hole in the wall where the bullet landed. He said nothing, though I could tell there were unspoken words hanging between us. Before I could say anything else, Romero touched the brim of his hat with two fingers and moved for the open door.

"Can I ride to the hospital with him?" I asked of his retreating back.

The sheriff half-turned toward me, his expression unreadable. "Better make it quick. Though that means you'll be stuck in the hospital until the storm clears out."

My shoulders sloped downward.

"That's all right," I said. "I don't want Finn to be alone when he wakes up. And after tonight, I could use the break."

Chapter Twenty-Six

The smell of roasting chicken and garlic filled Mistbrook Manor. My mouth salivated as I basted the bird, putting it back in the oven to get tender before the Wardens got here. Since asking the group over for a celebratory "we survived the doom of two killers" dinner, I had spent the day cleaning and cooking in preparation.

"That bird looks overdone."

Theo, on the other hand, spent the day complaining every chance he got. While I sweated buckets preparing a meal for five, plus the cat, he was lounging on the kitchen counter with his paw dipped into a bowl of whipped cream, licking it off as he continued to bombard me with his incessant comments. Either the potatoes were too mashed, or the roasted vegetables weren't roasted enough, or the blueberry pie wasn't blue enough. No matter what I did, it earned a scornful remark from the changeling.

I knew he was nervous about having people over at the house, so I let most of his comments slide off my back. If I was truthful, I was shaking in my boots as well. This was the first dinner party I hosted since...well, ever.

I tossed the salad I had cut up ahead of time and ran a mental inventory of all that was left to be done. The manor was in pretty decent shape, and that was with me being gone for two days while Finn recovered. I waited for the doctors to announce that he was out of the woods and well on his way to getting better, before finally saying goodbye to my makeshift bed in the hospital waiting room. When I went to see him after he woke up, I cried like a little baby. I wasn't sure if the tears were because he was alive, or from the disbelief of what had happened. Under normal circumstances, I'd have been embarrassed, but Finn didn't blink an eye. We both realized how surreal what we went through had been.

And he didn't even know the extent of what happened after he passed out.

For now, things were back to normal. Daisy and Arthur were behind bars and awaiting trial, though I doubted they'd be getting off, since the Whitmores hired the finest group of lawyers to take down the people responsible for their son's death. It was a bittersweet ending. On the one side, I was pleased to see the cousins in jail. No one should be pardoned for murder. On the other, I didn't know what I would do if I was in their place.

There was one silver lining to the entire terrible fiasco—the Whitmore family had their own legal battles to fight. The sheriff in Fine Bay was gearing up for a massive case to persecute the family for burying the hit-and-run. Last I heard through the Grim Wardens grapevine was that other cases of misconduct were popping up all over the place, from here to King City. Many people came forward to uncover the nasty truths behind the Whitmore fortune.

It would be interesting to see how it all unfolded.

Deep down, I hoped the family would get what they deserved for everyone they hurt. Especially for what Charles did to Greg. Though I guess he'd paid for it with his life already.

I folded the raw silk-cotton napkins I dug out from storage, and tied a ribbon around each one for the place settings. My breathing sped up as I thought about this weekend and the ceremony I offered to host for anyone willing to attend. It was a spur-of-the-moment idea that unfolded and transformed into an entire fiasco, yet one I was glad I thought of. It had been years since Greg's death, but the situation was different now—we knew what had happened to him, and the man finally got his justice. When I suggested a renewed memorial, I didn't think anyone would want to take part in it. After all, Greg's fiancée was in jail and most of his friends and family were in Fine Bay. Which was why I was so surprised when I received more than two dozen e-mails from people replying to my call-out on the town's events website.

Even Samuel, the mechanic, confirmed his attendance. He said after all he'd done to muck up the investigation, he wanted to make amends. It was a big step for a man who got off scot-free for what, in my opinion, was a colossally selfish act. But people did terrible things under pressure.

I blanched, thinking of Daisy and Arthur.

Horrible, terrible things.

I checked the time once more and turned the oven off, so the chicken had time to rest before everyone got here. If I hurried, I could actually put makeup on for a change, since I hadn't gone to the trouble of getting ready in forever. This evening, I opted for a casual dress in a forest green that brushed past my knees and floated when I spun. It made me giddy every time I took a step to feel the fabric drape against my skin. With my hair up in a loose up-do, I could barely recognize myself in the mirror. Though I had to admit, I cleaned up all right. Even Theo paid me a compliment—a rare occasion.

I tried not to think about *why* I was putting so much effort into my appearance, since it obviously wasn't for the Wardens' sake. Or not all of them.

A flash of movement caught my attention out of the corner of my eye. I rubbed my forehead in exasperation. "Theo! Get your nasty little paws out of the butter this instant!"

I reached for a tea towel hanging on the oven door and rushed for the cat. At this rate, the dinner might not survive before the guests arrived. I had better get a move on, starting with the rascal changeling currently causing havoc in the kitchen.

I couldn't afford for anything to ruin this evening. My eyes kept returning to the clock on the wall. If I hurried it up, I could probably squeeze in a magic session with the roses and frolic in the backyard with my wings out. Fairy knew I needed some magic today.

Glasses clinked as Ellie and Rosemary cheered over their empty plates. The dinner had gone off as a great success thus far, with everyone enjoying the meal enough to ask for seconds. To my right, Finn leaned on his elbows and listened to Mortimer recount his last appointment at the bank in a theatrical manner. The girls had given up on trying to hear over Mortimer's bouts of monologue, and had taken to their own conversation, which seemed to involve a whole lot of drinking.

My lips stretched into a smile, watching them.

It was a wonder I waited so long to have people over; this wasn't half bad.

Something stabbed my ankle under the long oak dinner table, and I winced. Rolling my eyes, I picked up a piece of chicken from my plate and tossed it on the floor. Theo caught the meat before it touched the hardwood, devouring it in a sloppy mess before looking up at me for more. I giggled.

"I take it you like the bird now," I whispered, as I gave him a second helping.

The cat scarfed it down, his whiskers twitching. Since he couldn't reply with everyone here, he settled for giving me a death glare and what I assumed was the cat version of flipping me the bird. Theo's tail rose high in the air, and he turned on his heels to point it at me before stomping down the length of the table to someone else's feet. There, he proceeded to rub his head against Mortimer's leg until the old man poked his hand under to give the cat a chicken leg to chew on.

The scoundrel.

I shook my head and returned my focus to the table and the dinner participants. The Wardens were truly in their element tonight, all hand gestures and belly laughs that trailed long after a joke ended. I wondered how much of that had to do with the case we solved that—according to them—was the toughest they'd faced thus far.

Apparently, it earned me extra points as my first case for the secret society, and helped forego the initiation. I didn't want to ask what the initiation would have been had I not helped bring Daisy and Arthur—and Charles—to justice. Knowing this bunch, it was likely bizarre.

"What's on your mind?"

I bristled, my attention returning to the room at the sound of Finn's whispered words. Turning to face him, I squeezed the napkin on my lap tightly. "I was thinking about how funny life is," I said. "Last month, if you told me I'd be having dinner with a secret society of undertakers, I'd have laughed in your face."

"It is an odd group," Finn admitted. "You fit right in, though."

I jabbed an elbow in his side, earning me a deep chuckle that made my skin flush hot. "Are you saying I'm odd, Finn O'Malley?"

"Definitely. But in a good way," he replied.

His eyes gleamed, the effect mesmerizing me instantly. To catch Finn in a good mood was rare, and it reminded what a great guy he could be when he wasn't trying to push people away. It was strange how long it took me to see that we were not so different, me and Finn. We both put walls up to shut people out as a way to protect ourselves from having the past repeat. And we both mourned people we loved, albeit for different reasons.

I didn't know where my road with the Wardens would lead, but one thing was for certain—I was glad it involved Finn O'Malley.

"Hey, do you think I could talk to you for a second?" he asked. "Alone."

My heart skittered against my ribcage like a wild animal caught in a trap. I bit down on my tongue before I could say something embarrassing, and instead nodded quickly. Skin burning, I rubbed my clammy palms over the skirt of my dress and grabbed my plate, standing up.

"I think I'll put a pot of tea on," I announced.

As soon as I spoke, Finn said, "I'll help you out."

Both of us pretended not to see three pairs of eyes watching us walk out of the dining room and head for the kitchen. I kept my steps light, padding down the hallway with precision to avoid falling flat on my face. My legs had suddenly lost their bones. I floated on a cloud all the way to the kitchen with Finn on my heels.

When we entered, I walked to the stove and put on a fresh pot, even though the tea was an excuse to talk to Finn without the others.

As the water bubbled and boiled, I turned around, praying my cheeks weren't the color of the living room carpet. I wasn't sure what it was, but ever since the hospital, I couldn't get Finn out of my head. And I didn't mind it one bit.

"So," I said.

"So," Finn echoed.

We stared at each other, our gazes locked and our eyes unblinking. There was a weight in the air that wasn't there before, and it made my knees buckle. Suddenly, the dress I wore suffocated me. Was it me, or was it hotter here than before? It must be because the stove is on. Surely.

The sound of boisterous laughter ripped the moment in half, bringing us both back instantly.

I cleared my throat. "What did you want to speak to me about?"

"I wanted to thank you," Finn said. "For saving my life and for staying with me. It meant a lot."

"You don't have to thank me for that. I did what anyone else would do in my position."

Finn laughed. "No one else would weather a storm in a hospital waiting room for someone they only met a week ago," he argued. "It was a big deal to me, what you did. I wanted to make sure you knew I appreciated it."

I grinned like a fool, all my teeth showing.

"I still don't understand why the Foxglove had no effect on you," he said.

My body temperature dropped drastically. "I probably didn't drink as much of the tea as you did," I lied.

"Probably," Finn mused. "Or you're a witch."

I chuckled awkwardly at his poorly positioned joke. *If you only knew,* I wished to say. But I kept my mouth shut and my eyes on Finn, trying not to ruin the moment. I could never tell him about who I was, of course, and yet it was nice to pretend that there was a future where I could be completely honest with Finn. One where—

"Do you want to go to dinner with me sometime?"

Finn's question caught me off guard. I crossed my arms, then uncrossed them and let them drop to the sides lamely. My gaze met his. "We're having dinner now."

"I meant outside. In a restaurant. Without three undertakers in tow," Finn said teasingly. "But if not, I completely understand."

"Yes!" I yelped. Catching myself, I sniffled and corrected, saying, "I mean, sure. That sounds lovely."

Finn's shoulders slumped as a head of short dark curls popped into our periphery. Ellie stood framed by the kitchen doorway, her brows slanted in curiosity. She looked between Finn and me, grinning from ear to ear. "Mortimer is wondering if anyone wants to play Death or Dare."

"Don't you mean Truth or Dare?" I asked.

Finn shook his head. He leaned in close, and my blood pressure spiked. "Not the way we play it," he explained. "This is the mortician's version of the game. Quite fun, if not a tad over the top."

"Mortimer? Over the top?" Ellie exclaimed. "Never."

We waited until the tea was done, and the two helped me carry the cups into the living room, where Mortimer had already set the seats up for the game. It was essentially the same as the original, but instead of telling a truth, you had to name the most obscure death you could think of. It could be anything in history, but the trick was that it had to involve an interesting fact either about the victim or the killer or both. Everyone racked their brains to outdo one another, since no one wished to be on the receiving end of a dare.

Undertakers could get creative with those.

The rest of the evening passed in a blur of jokes and warm conversation over tea by the fire. By the time everyone departed, I was too exhausted to move, let alone clean up. Deciding to leave the mess for tomorrow,

I tasked Theo with picking our movie for the evening while I spent a few short moments with the flowers.

My body ached to use my magic. What happened in the flower shop reminded me that I wasn't like everyone else, no matter how I tried to blend in. I was a fairy, and it was time to stop running away from my true self. Especially when it came to abilities that could help others around me.

I skipped down the cobblestone path leading to the back garden, my chest swelling with anticipation. Tonight, it was feeding the roses, but tomorrow I would come up with a plan to get back in touch with my magic, one day at a time.

Rounding the side of the house, I approached the roses, stopping dead in my tracks.

"No!" I whisper-shouted. "No, no, no."

I dropped to my knees in the dirt in front of shriveled, dead flowers. My fingers cradled the dried-up stems, thorns cutting my skin until blood welled on the scratches. My vision flickered with tears. I blinked them away, my neck straining to see the remainder of the garden.

Every flower was gone.

Fear clawed at my rigid spine. This was not an act of nature. The flowers were fine when I checked on them this morning. Better than fine, actually, they were thriving. Which meant someone did this. Someone came into my garden and killed my beautiful roses.

A hot lump formed in my throat.

This was a message. There was no denying it and no hiding from the truth before me. I trembled, my arms hugging the dead flowers to my chest. The Prince of the Shadow Court knew where I was, and he was coming back to claim what was his.

Me, and everyone in my life, were in terrible danger.

Right when I thought things were getting back to normal, my past had to catch up with me. I stood up, facing the looming shape of Mistbrook Manor over-looking the cliffs. Rolling my shoulders back, I uncurled my fingers and let the roses fall to the ground.

Let him come, I thought.

I was not the girl that ran from him and Fairy with her tail between her legs and her wings clipped. This time, I had something to fight for. I had a life here in Orchard Hollow, and I would be damned if I let anyone take it away from me.

"You want me?" I asked of the night. "Come and get me. I'm ready for you."

My magic surged to the surface, wings popping out in all their sparkly glory. I narrowed my gaze on the hori-zon. No matter what the prince thought, there would be no fairy funerals on my watch. I would claw my way to keep the life I built. I was magic, and I wasn't afraid. I would never be afraid again.

With slow, deliberate steps, I made my way back to the manor and slipped inside, locking the deadbolt behind me. Tomorrow, I fight, but tonight was reserved for celebration. With that, I left my worries in the garden and walked to the living room to join Theo. Troubles would have to wait. I had a movie to watch and a changeling to argue with.

A.N. Sage is a bestselling, award-winning author of mystery and fantasy novels. She has spent most of her life waiting to meet a witch, vampire, or at least get haunted by a ghost. In between failed seances and many questionable outfit choices, she has developed a keen eye for the extra-ordinary.

A.N. spends her free time reading and binge-watching television shows in her pajamas. Currently, she resides in Toronto, Canada with her husband who is not a creature of the night and their daughter who just might be.

A.N. Sage is a Scorpio and a massive advocate of leggings for pants.

For more books and updates:

www.ansage.ca

Connect on social media:

Facebook Group:
facebook.com/groups/945090619339423/
Instagram:
instagram.com/a.n.sage/
TikTok:
tiktok.com/@ansagewrites
YouTube:
youtube.com/c/ANSageWrites